AIDS, Love's Fight.

The Love Story of Fawn

By Frank Julian

ISBN 0-7414-6266-4

Printed in the United States of America

Published November 2010

INFINITY PUBLISHING
1094 New DeHaven Street, Suite 100
West Conshohocken, PA 19428-2713
Toll-free (877) BUY BOOK
Local Phone (610) 941-9999
Fax (610) 941-9959
Info@buybooksontheweb.com
www.buybooksontheweb.com

Chapter One

Thinking Back

"I need a miracle, God. AIDS. Me. Why must my life end now, like this?" Father Francis sighed breathlessly from the depths of his soul as he lay in his hospital bed as pale as the white sheets that nearly enshroud him. He is suffering from the complications of HIV/AIDS, pneumonia has caused his lungs to be filled with fluid and a fast growing cancer is eating him alive. He's waiting for his minister friend to arrive at any moment. Francis had a plan, he is going to make things right. So many thoughts were channeling through his mind muddling with the fear and the depression that were once rooted there a long time ago. Settling down into his hospice bed he thought back to when it all really began, when one event triggered another after the church board ruled on an important decision.

In the stillness of that night long ago, the only sound that could be heard for those willing to listen was his heart quietly breaking. He could actually feel the stillness in the air, feeling so alone and vulnerable. This was not the first time Francis would cry out to God and it wouldn't be the last. A falling tear moistened his pale blue shirt cuff. The sorrow in his aching heart cried out to be relieved under-standing each tear is carefully counted by the same God who lit a million stars with one glance and scatters galaxies with a single nod. Francis sobbed as he prayed regarding his lifelong vow to serve God. He admitted his feelings of love for God had waned at times and confessed his feelings for Sister Margaret or Maggie as he called her, were deeper and more meaningful than casual friendship. A sense of confusion overwhelmed him as he poured out his heart in prayer. He wondered what will become of him, his parish and possibly his career as a Catholic priest. He looked around the gloomy monotony of his study in the old inner city parish of Saint Rita's church rectory. The dark paneled walls and dreary brown furniture with matching threadbare carpet made Francis feel as if he'd been buried alive in a grave from which there was no escape.

Francis rose from his knees and gazed into the full length framed mirror near the heavy wooden door, "Who are you?" he asked the disheveled reflection staring back at him. The moderately built frame and sandy brown hair were familiar but his trademark smiling hazel eyes were dull. The pain of his reflection squeezed his heart sending scorching tears flowing from his scarlet reddened eyes.

Chapter Two

Where It All Began

Inside the parish hall at St. Rita's, Angela Harrid smoothed her chestnut shoulder length hair wishing she were anywhere else on the planet as she prepared for the battle she is certain will transpire after she calls the parish executive board meeting to order. At the top of the agenda next to Roman Numeral One is the name Father Francis, with the words "Incident in Church". This incident occurred between Father Francis and Sister Margaret and was witnessed by one of the board members. It doesn't matter how innocent the embrace was, appearances can go a long way in creating scuttlebutt in the collective consciousness of the parishioners.

This is the hot and spicy stuff affluent socialite the Widow Henrietta Bridges, loved to fuel. With an already overactive imagination and so little excitement in her everyday life, titillating fantasy is a most welcome pastime for the church busybody. Unfortunately since the death of her tender-hearted husband, Mr. Cyprian Maxwell Bridges, II, who was the church board chair, well loved and known as a very generous man, she'd taken it upon herself to gather all the goodwill he nurtured over the many years and cashed it in to influence the daily workings of the parish. A storm was brewing on the horizon for years. Father Francis, whose legendary energetic levels slowed down to a snail's pace was worn out from fighting the political battles that Widow Bridges keenly cultivated through her manipulation and her coercion.

"It's downright indecent, a priest embracing a nun in such a familiar manner right in the church before the crucifix," Widow Bridges sneered through her thin, colorless lips turned downward with just the proper amount of righteous indignation. "I understand you're upset but we must calmly discuss this and not jump to any conclusions, Mrs. Bridges," Angela showed no hint of anxiety in her plea, having experienced more than one of Widow Bridges' outbursts, "I have spoken with Father Francis about this and..."

"Everyone knows your relationship with Father Francis," the widow loudly cut in, "from the time you were a child running around this parish in your dingy little dress and smudged face." Widow Bridges pointed her personal attack in Angela's direction attempting to undercut the chair-woman's authority.

Angela's brilliant brown eyes blazed and her throat ached as she struggled to choke back the words her lips begged to say. At this instant she appeared much taller than her tiny five foot frame, "The fact that I was raised by a single mother without many resources is irrelevant to this meeting. It's true that Father Francis is like a father to me. I needed a dad but that's precisely what makes me the perfect go-between to help resolve this misunderstanding."

"What misunderstanding? There's an eyewitness to this incident!" a self satisfied smirk was apparent on Widow Bridges' round face as her gray eyes showed a hint of a twinkle.

"It doesn't sound very good, Angela," Charlie interjected with his usual timid voice trying to appease everyone. Angela's anger diminished as she turned to face Charlie

Matthews, who was dressed in the same pressed brown suit he's faithfully worn to church every Sunday since she could remember, "I know, Mr. Matthews, but that's the point of this meeting; to clear things up so if there are any decisions to be made, we have the facts and not just conjecture."

Widow Bridges turned her head away for a moment intimating her disgust at not being taken seriously. Angela knew it was more about a power struggle than any pertinent information when it came to the elderly woman's distorted agenda. Her obvious dislike for Sister Margaret now only made the fight that much sweeter for her.

"Is it true that Father Francis and Sister Margaret were found in the church embracing?" Sister Mary David asked without the slightest hint of judgment in her voice. Sister Mary David was one to always believe the best of everyone; having taken her vows as a nun a year ago, she's yet to become jaded by life in the struggling inner city parish where sin is as familiar as breathing. "Yes, it's true; however, you must remember that Father Francis and Sister Margaret were friends before they even took their vows. They actually met each other first when they enrolled in nursing school at the same time," Angela explained to the kind hearted younger sister who listened intensely.

"You see, that's exactly my point; they are intimate with one another." Widow Bridges said smugly as she tucked a wisp of gray hair back into the tight bun on top of her head.

· "Why you...", Angela pressed her full lips together to thwart the fury of words yearning to emerge, "they are NOT intimate with each other and you need to be more careful when you use such a word in the world where the language is constantly changing. People could get the wrong impression."

"If they don't want to give the wrong impression maybe they should stop pressing up against each other – and of all places, in the church," Widow Bridges sneered, again with that grin, that smirk of self satisfied animosity.

"In times of sadness and happiness, they've been true friends who've supported one another. I believe them and trust them when they say the call to fulfill God's work on Earth is always placed above any of the feelings they might have for each other." Angela said defensively giving the appearance of a small general in a dark business suit and high heels.

"Ah, ha! So you admit you think that there are feelings between them!"

"Of course there are feelings between them but you pointing and shaking your finger at them doesn't make them sinners. It makes you a gossip!" Angela paused for a moment to regain her composure. While Widow Bridges' mouth was still hanging open, playing the part of the shocked innocent, Angela resumed her argument, "Why is it that the entire parish knew about all of this before the board had any idea? It's common knowledge that anything having to do with the church is discussed by the board first before talking about it outside this room so that we might be prayerful and considerably thoughtful about how God would have us handle any given situation." Trying to deflect the negative attention, Widow Bridges turned and said, "So then, why were they hugging?" using her most seasoned squeaky and sophisticated tone of voice. "If you had taken just one quick moment to ask before blabbing it all around, you'd have learned that Sister Margaret was dealing with a family tragedy which left her devastated. Father Francis was merely consoling his friend and colleague."

"So that is why Sister Margaret went away?" Charlie asked shaking his bald head as he recalled her absence.

Sister Mary David responded in the gentle way of a nun who has comforted many lost souls, "She came to me for prayer and didn't want to share it with the whole church at the time because she felt so off-kilter due to the sudden nature of it all."

"I had no idea", Charlie quietly said with true compassion in his voice as Angela resounded at the same time, "Between us and these four walls, Mrs. Bridges, I know you had something to do with the rumor flying around at the time that Sister Margaret was on leave because of a 'personal' issue that needed to be 'taken care of', so to speak! This along with your comments over the months about an intimate relationship between Father Francis and Sister Margaret have done nothing but put unsubstantiated doubts and speculation in the minds of the parishioners. You knew what kind of seed you were sowing."

"I will not tolerate these kinds of accusations, young lady! As a matter of fact, the very nature of your own relationship with Father Francis clouds your judgment in these matters and I think it's high time you step down as board chair!" Widow Bridges slapped her hand down on the worn oak table for emphasis, her hard gray eyes scanning the room for signs of agreement.

"Does anyone else here feel the same way as Mrs. Bridges?" Angela asked with humility in her voice. Her high-powered position in the business world has taught her to read the nuances of people's faces and to know when to back off. She's sure now that Mrs. Bridges had alienated herself from most, if not all, of the board members with her outrageous antics. The supportive response of the other eight board members is reassuring to Angela as she turned their attention to and opened discussion of the upcoming mission trip to Africa.

While the meeting continued, Francis prayed alone in his study, feeling quite small as he pondered the insignificance of his life and personal struggles compared to the expanse of history in a world held in balance on the tip of God's finger.

To God, Francis was like a wildflower sown in rich soil sprouting with an inquisitive nature. As an adolescent boy, refreshed over time by the watering of a servant's soul, grew into a young man who desired to heal those who were hurting. He grew into maturity unorthodox by religious standards but imperative by God's standards. Now, once again he was languishing in a spiritual drought but in the mind of God, Francis is simply suffering more spiritual growing pains as he endured the dry valley in which he now finds himself entrenched. All Francis could breathe was a desperate whispered prayer as he fell upon his knees, "Jesus, please help me. Jesus, please."

Closing his swollen eyes, Francis wandered back in time to St. Julian's College Campus when he first met Maggie at the midweek mass celebration after registering into the Nursing College. How could he know that this stage in his life would be pivotal to his decision to become a priest in lieu of a practicing nurse or that a fellow nursing student would become the most integral part of his future? The mass concluded and folks were meandering toward their destinations when Francis noticed a strikingly beautiful girl with long dark hair across the room. He made his way through the crowd smiling and shaking hands and offering greetings but when he reached the object of his attention, she appeared to look through him as if he were invisible when he offered his hand out to her. Slightly embarrassed, he moved on to the next parishioner, barely missing a beat and thought, "she's obviously not interested in me; she must be one of those stuck-up girls only interested in herself."

How could he know she didn't notice his extended hand because she was so captivated by his smile? Maggie had never seen anyone smile so broadly and sincerely as the young man who stood in front of her. His entire presence exuded love and caring, it was so different from the men Maggie had met. As he walked away, she thought, "He probably didn't even notice me as anything more than a face in the crowd."

Francis heard Father Paul, the Director of Admissions, calling to him, "Come here, son, there's someone I'd like you to meet," Francis turned to see Father Paul waving him over to where he was standing with the beautiful dark-haired girl, "Frank Galliano, this is Maggie Iskra, I understand the two of you will be attending nursing school together."

"Really?" Maggie said with a slightly surprised look, "I hadn't realized there would be a man in the class."

"Don't worry, I don't bite," he said with a grin noticing how her dark eyes glimmered in the sunlight shining through the stained glass windows.

"Oh, I'm so sorry. I didn't mean it like that; it's just that there aren't many male nurses around that I know of."

"Don't worry, I hear that a lot. I plan to break the mold and open the floodgates for men all over the world to become nurses. Don't be surprised if within twenty years all nurses are men!" he laughed. Maggie couldn't help but notice how his eyes danced when he smiled making her feel so comfortable and warm loving.

"Well, I hope they don't put me out of a job," she chuckled.

"Why don't the two of you get to know each other?" Father Paul asked, "You never know when you might need a study partner," he added as he walked away.

Francis felt an immediate sense of familiarity with Maggie coupled with the attraction he felt since his first glimpse of her across the room. Maggie thought Francis was genuinely friendly even though he was so remarkably attractive.

"Can I buy you a cup of coffee?" Francis asked with his contagious smile.

"I would love that," Maggie answered as she took his arm.

"I was wrong about her," Francis thought as he led the way, "she's not stuck-up at all."

They talked and laughed over coffee for what turned into hours. Maggie couldn't remember ever meeting a young man so cordial, sweet in nature, and down right fun in a wholesome kind of way. As a young Catholic woman, she found this to be a delightful contrast to the machismo of the day. The inner strength she sensed in him as they became friends was palpable to a young woman who was serious minded about her own call to do God's work wherever that call might lead.

Francis within grew tired of being just a nice guy; there was nothing glamorous or intriguing about that. Little did he know that Maggie was drawn in and she couldn't help being attracted to him, he was popular with everyone, even without trying to, he could make others laugh and defuse any situation with his easygoing and kind charisma; no one could stay mad for very long about anything around him. He made you want to get along with everyone. Maggie basked in his enthusiasm as they talked for hours about their hopes and dreams of their common career goal which they chose separately and for different reasons, hers being of a much more personal nature from an experience of personal loss.

Later in their relationship which led to the "incident in the church" Maggie described the loss of her teenage brother due to a horrific construction accident to Francis. She felt everyone let her brother down with respect to what modern medicine could have accomplished in saving him, she had an honest desire to be a part of the solution to the problem she bitterly felt contributed to her brother's death. Francis recalled lovingly wrapping his arms around her to ease her suffering simply by being there he said, "Remember the image of Mary standing strong at the foot of the cross? You remind me of her, you are going to make it." In that same moment of struggling with letting her brother go, a strong bond between her and Francis formed out of the ashes of her grief. A warm feeling perpetually enters her heart whenever she thinks back to that day, about how Francis took her face in his strong hands and his warm hazel eyes smiled down on her, kissing her sweetly and when he hugged her, she felt his tears of empathy on her cheek. Mere words cannot express what can't be spoken but only felt when in the presence of someone who genuinely and truly cares.

Chapter Three

Love's Rude Awakening

The memory of that time brought Francis to his knees as he waited to hear something, anything, regarding the board's reaction to the incident. He had no qualm about whatever God's will would be, Francis was more than happy to stay under His care and protection no matter where the final decision placed him but he felt obligated to pray for each board member asking that they listen with open minds and hearts and he prayed the truth would be revealed without twisting the facts or any fabrication. No matter what, he will always feel the same with absolutely no regret, ever; he wouldn't change a thing if he could go back in time.

Francis' prayers then led his thoughts to roam to his father, Anthony Galliano, Francis thought of the brave stories from World War II that his dad told him long ago. Anthony was a Surgical Technician in a MASH unit on the front line during World War II in Italy. His father saw first hand the horrific deeds of a bloody war yet he managed to carry on with peace of mind, like in the eye of a hurricane, he saved many lives which scattered across his path in the process. When the war ended and Anthony became a US citizen, he turned in the surgical scissors and picked up the hair cutting shears to open his own barbershop in the small town with striped barber pole, flowers out in front, games and treats for the kids and even a pony chair for the children to sit in when they were getting their hair cut. Francis could literally smell the lavender hair tonic that his father would shake and gingerly pour onto his customer's head clipping away and while the waiting patrons chatted about the weather and told the latest joke, Frankie was busy sweeping hair and folding towels dreaming of the day when he would be grown up and following in his father's footsteps healing the sick and injured people while remaining calm with God right at his side at all times.

The escape down memory lane relieved Francis for a time as his reflections vanished into thin air quicker than they had arrived. He was back to facing the difficult circumstances of the moment. The board knew very well that Father Francis and Sister Margaret have known each other for years and pursued their nursing careers together. Sister Margaret was assigned to this parish after Father Francis first arrived; it was an old parish in a dilapidated part of town with run down houses and mainly old people, Francis and Maggie loved and respected the old people. Working together felt understandably comfortable not unlike their former nursing days when they dreamed about their mutual callings to serve God through the ministry of the Church. The connection between them was built upon service to others. Through God's grace they were each privileged to witness His hand in the other's life, they healed those who suffered through the miracle of modern medicine and the touch of loving hands.

It's true in recent months, Francis and Maggie relied on each other more as they prayed about the parish losing its way to the mundane processes of everyday church life. The programs, board meetings and services were filled with busy work and lacked a sense of mission. They both wished younger people would become interested enough to join them and help out, that was one of the reasons why they were so looking forward to the upcoming mission trip to

Africa. They also hoped it would rekindle something spiritual in them and upon their return, light a fire in the parishioners and draw new blood.

One incident of finding solace in each other's arms during a moment of consolation, comfort in a time of grief should certainly not be the single cause for poor church morale. Francis could feel the demons of depression taking him down again playing that broken record of bitter remorse over and over again; feeling the sense of loss for what once was a passion aglow for God alone. This old parish does need the vitality of someone who can represent the hope of Jesus Christ in a dismal world but he's lost count or maybe stopped counting how many parishioners have recently died or left the church and felt he's a failure to God, himself and the flock he's responsible in leading to greener pastures. Privately, he is desperately hoping the greener pastures might somehow be found in Africa.

A knock at the door broke his concentration and he flew down the stairs to answer it. He glanced out the window and saw Maggie, her thick brown hair pulled back from her heart shaped face, standing in the faint glow of the dimly lit doorway. He's never been any good at hiding his delight in seeing her, she gives him strength especially when he's feeling down and he always looked forward to her encouragement; her brown eyes twinkled up at him when he opened the door and greeted her, inviting her in.

"I have news from Angela, I spoke with her after the board meeting ended," Maggie said with a slight hesitation in her voice trying to hide her utter dismay.

Tell me, please, what did the board say?"

"You can go to Africa, Francis," she said with feigned excitement, "But...."

"But what?"

"But I can't go with you."

"What? No! How can I possibly go without you?" Francis responded softly and honestly as he motioned her into the sitting room, "I didn't see this coming."

"You must go, Francis. We already know God has something for you to do there," she chided with an authority in her voice and trying to sound cheerful.

"I suppose so."

"I thought God had something there for me, too." Maggie wiped away a tear hoping Francis didn't see it, "They asked Father Patrick to go with you, he'll be a wonderful addition to the trip," she said with a smile, hoping to bring comfort to him.

Maggie didn't have the heart to tell him that she wouldn't be there when he returned from Africa. Unknown to him, his mission trip to Africa was contingent upon her reassignment, she knew the disappointing news of her sanction was all he could handle right then. She didn't want anything to get in the way of his focus on Africa. They fell silent for a moment then Maggie took his hand in hers and encouraged him to walk with her. She knew her transfer was permanent and she doesn't care now what it looks like to anyone else as they held hands. Their spark was undeniably still there. Francis was so distracted by the news he didn't even remember to think of being self conscious at the prospect of being seen. Even as her heart was breaking she tried to cheer him up by recollecting funny stories and experiences from their lives as students and new nurses.

"I'd forgotten about that," he laughed as she reminded him about one of his first visits as a new nurse. Maggie giggled remembering, "And after asking the patient to change into what you thought was a dressing gown but…"

"Was actually a pillow case I'd mistakenly given him and when I came back in…"

"Being the obedient patient that he obviously was," she chimed in chuckling.

"I found him sitting there with nothing but a pillow case over his head!"

"I can't believe you kept your composure."

"I didn't. I backed out of the room for a moment to get myself together", Francis admitted with a sheepish grin while Maggie burst into laughter.

His expression suddenly turned to sadness as reality set in. He wouldn't be hearing her enduring laugh for quite some time but he learned a long time ago not to let his own personal agenda get in the way of God's will. Maggie and Francis or Sister Margaret and Father Francis long ago came to a mutual understanding that the calling of their lives must take precedence. Francis could always tell when Maggie was feeling sentimental about their relationship because she would call him "Father" to bring a subtle reminder into the conversation of both of their callings that God's work was to be the focus. As much as they love each other, their first loves are the same love, Jesus. Can the two loves coexist?

They never have to say it to each other but there is a godly affection between them that translates into something even deeper than what the world could possibly understand on a physical plane; it's spiritual in nature, they understood they could lean on each other and God. Francis knew he was having difficulty in not allowing his feelings for Maggie to surface and as much as he hated to admit it to himself, a time apart from one another may not be such a bad idea but Francis doesn't know their separation could be permanent.

Chapter Four

Father Patrick and Love's Question

Father Patrick's arrival was welcomed by Francis, who still felt like he'd been hit by an emotional locomotive. Father P, as he called him was a white haired, ruddy faced older Irish gentleman, dear mentor and friend. Francis also considered it a great compliment, the older priest's willingness to come out of retirement to fill Maggie's shoes on the trip to Africa bringing with him his wise counsel and companionship. Francis looked forward with anticipation to a consort who was known for lifting the load of fellow priests through his attentive ear and seasoned manner.

"It's so great to see you, Father P", for the first time since yesterday's bad news Francis smiled and felt happy as if he'd forgotten how.

"It's been a while since anyone's called me Father P," he said leaning back and looking down the bridge of his nose and with a big smile embraced Francis like a father hugs a natural born son.

"Might I add you haven't changed a bit," Francis remarked.

"Oh, no, not a bit! Other than a few too many pounds and a few well-earned wrinkles, I'm the same as ever but let me have a look at you, m'boy, I'll say you've lost a few pounds and appears you could use some sleep, as well."

"I'm very excited about this trip to Africa. So many people there are in desperate need of our help", Francis asked, "Are you ready to see Africa?"

"I saw Africa many years ago before I became a priest, Francis," he said with an enlightened timbre in his voice and a cheerful laugh.

"Really?" Francis said looking somewhat puzzled, "you've never mentioned it before."

"Oh there are a few things this old Irish priest hasn't told you about."

"Well, we'll have a long plane trip to tell stories and catch up," Francis winked.

"You wouldn't be insinuatin' that this ol' Irishman is prone to telling tall tales, would'ya now?" Father P said as one eyebrow goes straight up in the air and he danced a little jig looking a bit like a large leprechaun.

"Oh, certainly not, Father. I know your vows would circumvent any inclination you might have to not tell the truth, the whole truth and nothing but the truth," Francis said reminding Father P he recalled more about the old priest than he might want remembered.

"I see, you're trying to hold me to a higher standard of our legal system from which I have very fond memories as a prosecutor turned priest," he said as Father Francis led him into the library and set his bags down next to the stairs, Francis said, "From finger pointer to a man of the cloth. What was God thinking?"

"I can tell you what God was thinking. He figured He had converted the old Christian slayer, Saul, into the Apostle

Paul on the road to Damascus and looked for something even harder to tackle." They both laughed and continued to reminisce through dinner.

After dinner, they discussed their plans for the trip and the conversation came round to the reason why Father P was drafted to this particular post. Francis confided in Father P about his feelings for Maggie and how they'd actually courted in nursing school. He detailed the incident that caused the current firestorm in the parish. Father P assumed it was Francis' call to the priesthood that prevented the courtship from turning into marriage. But Francis corrected him and explained how he tried to scratch the itch of the God given assignment he had since birth to fulfill his divine destiny, that he did this by following in his father's footsteps through aiding the sick and suffering as a nurse in the medical field. Logically, he could be a nurse instead of a priest but as he became more formally interested in spiritual matters while attending the Catholic college he researched an order that combined a walk of faith with nursing skills. In 1930, Pope Pius XI named St. Camillus de Lellis (1550 – 1614), together with St. John of God, principal Co-Patron of nurses and of nurses' associations. Francis explained to Father P that this was an answer to a prayer for him because it was a way he could feel somehow connected to his father's military legacy and follow his own heart. He could be a priest and a nurse! Who would've thought that could happen?

"So, what about Maggie?" Father P asked with a hint of anxiety in his voice.

"I actually proposed but she didn't want to be the reason for getting in the way of my calling. She simply refused to consider marriage," Francis said with a crinkled brow, "I had the ring in my pant's pocket at Midnight Mass on Christmas Eve. I could almost feel it burning a hole in my pocket all through mass. When I asked her to marry me, she at first said "yes!" and then suddenly she said, 'oh, no! I do love you, Frankie, but I could never live with myself if I took you away from the priesthood!' in a way she chose the priest-hood for me. She closed the gap in my desire to become a priest."

"Francis, are you telling me you're having regrets about not marrying Maggie?"

"At the time I was focused on doing what I believed God wanted me to do. I was so excited about this priest nursing order. I'm sure Maggie sensed the enthusiasm in my spirit. She felt it was of God," Francis admitted.

"But that didn't make it any easier, did it?" Father P finished Francis' thought.

"No. But I've disciplined myself to suppress my earthly desires in order to fulfill a higher purpose. I desperately want my life to count for something in the long run, in an eternal kind of way. Living my life simply for myself and pursuing the American dream always seemed selfish and shortsighted to me," Francis hung his head in repose.

"And now, Francis?" asked Father P.

"Now I'm confused. I'm not sure why I don't feel passionate about my work the way I once did," Francis shared in sacred confidence.

"You know, Francis, we all have times when we question the call. It's happened to me as well," Father P said quietly.

"Really? That's hard to believe. Sometimes lately I feel like Peter after he denied Jesus", Francis said with dismay and looked up to see Father P's reaction.

"Why, are you up to three denials? Don't be so hard on yourself. I fought God tooth and nail when He chased me from one courtroom to another. But I couldn't escape because I kept seeing His face in the people I was prosecuting. I wouldn't let even the slightest offense be overlooked by the judge, I was a very diligent SOB, too, when it came to putting those slime balls away for the havoc they were wreaking in society. You see, I considered it a sacred honor to make sure those criminals knew how wrong they were. I didn't just want to put them away for as long as possible, I wanted to use the legal system to embarrass, harass, and persecute their pitiful little lives."

As Father P continued to share his conversion to the ways of Christ and the forgiveness that is the hallmark of Christendom, Francis understood that the narrow path of faith is sometimes dark and dangerous in a world where the wide path often loomed up to swallow the weak. Francis confessed he was feeling vulnerable just then but Father P assured him that the enemy was just trying to dull his sense of mission. After the discussion ended, the two men knelt together in agreement of their belief and prayed to rekindle their courage and passion for the long awaited trip to Africa. They asked God to create a new horizon of faith and a new season to turn the frozen lifeless winter into a satisfying spring of hope. As they fellow-shipped, Francis felt his icy heart begin to thaw as the light of the new day would bring him closer to stepping aboard the fueled jet plane bound for Africa ready to fly him to his sacred destiny for God.

Chapter Five

Francis' Emotional Journey and God's Plan

Early the next morning as the sun rose, Francis woke up in a cold sweat. He remembered a vivid dream where Widow Bridges was pointing the tip of a sword into his back as she made him walk the plank on a pirate ship while the crew, the church board, watched intensely, then just as he was ready to take his last step overboard, First Mate Angela spun the large wheel that steered the vessel simultaneously throwing old lady Bridges into the sea while tossing Francis back aboard with one flick of her wrist. He woke up just as he felt the thump of hitting the deck.

"What a silly dream!" Father Patrick couldn't help but laugh when Francis shared his dream at breakfast, "did she have an eye patch, Francis?" Father P grinned with delight.

"Of course not, it wouldn't be in character because she's all seeing, you know." Francis said with a nod as he tilted his head to one side.

"You really do need to get away, my friend, the stress of this whole situation is getting to you," Father P suggested.

"You don't have to tell me. But I admit, sometimes it feels like my crew wants to mutiny," Francis said half joking.

Father P leaned over with intention and said, "I can appreciate that son, but always remember that God is really the captain of the ship and He won't let anyone overthrow His command. Your life sails are blown by His ever changing winds and the tides of each season are guided by His pull of forgiveness and mercy."

"I'm so happy you're taking this trip with me, Father. I can't begin to tell you what a comfort your words are," Francis said as his voice cracked with sentiment.

"Don't mention it. After three months with me, you'll be singing a different tune," Father P said and offered up a toast with his teacup.

Francis sat back and smiled as he listened to the sound of Father Patrick's voice. You can hear the years of experience in the way he said each word with confidence and ease. It's as if he'd said them a million times before in another place and time. Francis wondered if he would ever reach that point in his walk of faith where he would be as comfortable in his own skin as his mentor and friend seemed to be.

As the morning drifted into the afternoon, he wondered how Maggie was coping with this most critical recent development. He knew how she had been preparing for months to make this first mission trip abroad successful and she must be extremely disappointed. Maggie was not only thinking about this temporary separation from Francis but was wondering how long it would last, if it would become a permanent separation. She felt vulnerable and quite alone and decided to call her brother, George. She was delighted at first to hear his voice and shared with him what currently transpired to throw her life off balance. As she spoke, listening to herself speak, she realized at that moment how much she depends on Francis. George knows they've always been there for each other and now at a critical point in her life, Maggie can't even share her sorrow with the one whom she wants to reach out to the most, Francis. George related to her predicament because he became quite close to Francis over the years, like a brother. Years ago when Francis agreed to perform George's wedding ceremony, his soon to be wife, Lisa laughingly stated, "Francis couldn't be the best man and perform the ceremony, too!" George loved to repeat that statement reminding Maggie of it whenever Francis' name became part of any conversation and she would always laugh.

"Cheer up, sis, God's got a plan, you know how I know? Because Francis was the only one ever who would eat your green coconut cream pie on St. Patrick's Day," George said with confidence in his voice. "Now that's true love! End of story!"

"I wish I could talk to him, George, about things, you know?" Maggie said with sadness in her voice. She's desperate to find out if Francis would be devastated by her reassignment when he found out or was he distracted by what God may have in store for him in Africa? She shared with George that she wondered if their relationship had become a crutch. Could it be they both relied too much on each other? She revealed that transferring to the new convent just might revitalize her spirit to serve others and rely upon God only. Then she shared her deepest feeling and concern with her brother, had she become confused in her feelings for Francis? Was the loss of her passion for the parish the result of their becoming too close to each other over the years thereby creating disillusionment? There are many questions she will be asking in the months ahead as she seeks to heal her hurting heart. By the time she finished talking with her brother, she felt almost better, renewed yet bittersweet, as if she'd been to confession. He quoted a verse to her from Chapter Five from the book of James, "therefore confess your sins one to another, and pray for each other that you may be healed". She hung up the phone with her burden feeling lighter, for that moment anyway.

She decided to write a letter to Francis and leave it in his study for him to find when he returned from Africa. She wanted to explain why she hadn't told him before about her reassignment and the difficulty and the pain it caused in not revealing it to him. At her desk the sunshine beamed through the windowpane gliding across her face and onto the blank page as she carefully penned her letter. She poured out her heart with every word and prudently laced her phrases with terms like 'God's will' and 'providence's plan' but in between the lines there were traces of her broken heart, a confession of feeling lost without him. She desperately tried to dismiss the impression of composing a love letter but her feelings were so strong. She couldn't hide anymore what was buried so deep inside of her, the words from her heart that had never been spoken before, her sentiment spilled out staining the paper with blotted ink mixed with her tears,

My dearest Francis,

By the time you read this letter you'll be returned from Africa, with all of the wondrous sights still fresh in your memory. I hope you felt my prayers, I petitioned God to multiply what He had in store for you to make up for the loss of me not being there with you as we originally planned. I write this letter before my own departure, knowing that you'll return with a new found resolve continuing to do God's work.

Yes, my dear Francis, as part of the negotiations Angela was advised to make as the Board Chair included my taking an assignment at a new convent in order to separate us. I so desperately wanted to tell you but was worried it would be more difficult for you to go to Africa without me while knowing that I would not be here when you got back. I must cling to the belief that somehow God has allowed this to happen for reasons we cannot understand. I don't know when or even if I will ever see you again.

I want to apologize for breaking your heart on Christmas Eve so many years ago. I know we've never talked about it since then. It was just after graduation, the night before Christmas Eve, we were working together in the local Catholic hospital emergency room, remember? I knew of and affirmed your planned enthusiastic proposal only to reverse my decision the next day. I want you to know it was never because I had second thoughts or doubts about my feelings for you. I have always loved you and always will. But I couldn't allow myself to be the one to get in the way of your call to the Order to become a priest and a nurse. I couldn't live with that. I want you to know that your decision to live a life of celibacy in the priesthood is the reason I became a nun, because I knew you would be the only one I would ever love. Please know that you'll always be a part of me. Always. I will draw nearer to God, as I know you, too will in the days to come.

Lovingly,

Magpie

She knew God had given her the courage to write this letter from the consolation of her brother's listening ear and attentive phone presence and she will always love George for that. Writing the letter was eerily reminiscent to when Maggie and Francis parted at unseen crossroads in their lives before, not sure if they would ever see each other again when they graduated from school and discussed noble careers in nursing. The cruelty of circumstance seems to be striking the same blow to them now.

Francis would later describe his early years of training for the priesthood as lonely ones. He decided at the time to focus on the duty he felt called to as a public health servant and a man of the cloth who visits the sick and brings healing to body and soul. In order to fill the hole left by Maggie and her turning down his marriage proposal, Francis dug deeper within himself to that which tugged at him since childhood, his faith. The faith he believed in was like a seed planted in him since birth and was watered and sprouted in the living room of his grandmother's house when he was a small lad no older than six or seven years of age. Her bedroom was like a chapel with religious statues and pictures in every place possible, his sense of solitude and safety there was all encompassing to him like the aroma of a fragrant perfume. He would sit at his grandmother's feet and she'd tell him about her youthful desire to become a nun but her mother had died in childbirth when she was twelve years old and she had to help raise and care for the family. Even at this young age, little Frankie knew there was something important for him to do when it comes to belonging to God; he is a child of God. The older women gathered at his grandmother's house every Wednesday afternoon at 1:00 PM to pray.

Alongside them, Frankie would kneel and pray. His budding love and respect for God at this tender age would give way to a lifelong dedication of trying to understand this magnificent obsession of true love. Even then he realized the joy he received back from giving God his undivided attention. This was a happiness that went far beyond a temporal fleeting moment transcending the mere tickle of one's own fancy. When most youngsters dreamt of flying faster than a speeding locomotive and jumping over tall buildings with a single bound, Frankie's head was full of questions and divine images usually reserved for older and wiser sages. As he grew into adolescence, this insightfulness was both marvelous and menacing because of the separation he felt from others. Quite often, it annexed him into the arms of a loving God who would never leave him or forsake him no matter how misunderstood he might have felt throughout his lifetime, and the times when it seemed like it was just him and God against the world.

The flip side to this is the fullness of a cup overflowing with compassion toward his fellow man that's both unusual and uncommon in a world dedicated to an individual's selfish pursuits. But for a boy growing up feeling special because of his connection to God yet misunderstood by the world which doesn't value such things, was a very narrow and often harrowing emotional journey. Growing up and learning to disregard the approval of man in order to fulfill a higher calling of service would be the mountain little Frankie would have to learn to climb, he believed it must be scaled alone, dangling him on one single rope between the devastation of rejection and the divine destiny of grace. This rope was Jesus Himself and Frankie securely tied it around his waist knowing this is the only way he would survive whatever the future held.

Chapter Six

Old Friends, Does God Have a Plan?

As Francis packed his bags for the departure tomorrow for Africa, Angela dropped by with news about his arrangements once he arrives there. "You're packing more than this I hope," Angela commented like a doting daughter pressing down what's already in his suitcase to make room for more. "You're going to need another suitcase, Father. When my mother died you promised her you'd take care of me, well, I'll never stop looking out for you."

"I really want to pack light," he said with certainty.

"It's okay to pack light for a week's vacation but you're going to be gone much longer. Really, you need to pack more clothes!" she said with a question on the tip of her tongue, "did you pack enough underwear?"

"I most certainly did, Angela", he said trying to hide the noticeable blush on his cheeks.

"I'm sorry, I just want to make sure you're going to be alright especially since Sister Maggie won't be there to keep an eye on you," she said, "I did the best I could, Father, to iron things out, I mean but that old Widow Bridges..."

"It doesn't matter, everything's for the best. God knows...."

Angela bit her tongue as she thought about this man she's come to know as a father and his complete unawareness of the permanence of his separation from Maggie. For his sake she promised Maggie her silence and was determined to keep her secret, she knows the time will come when he must learn the truth and Angela vowed to herself that she will be there with him when that time arrives. In a strange kind of way, even as a grown woman, she can't help but feel sadness like as if her parents were splitting up. She's known Father Francis since her early childhood and immediately felt a very close bond with Sister Maggie since her arrival here when Angela was still a child. Francis had no idea how many conversations the two women had over the years, woman to woman. Angela doesn't know how she would have made it without Maggie's kind and gentle leading guidance and reassurances with her, a young lady with many questions about the budding life of entering into womanhood. Angela made it through some very tumultuous years purely because they both had been there for her. Angela promised Maggie that she'd make arrangements for them to see each other once Francis learned the truth of Maggie's reassignment. She didn't exactly know how this would come about but she will make sure it does.

As Angela helped Francis bring his luggage downstairs for tomorrow morning's departure there was a knock at the door. The swirling fall breeze swung the door open almost pinning Angela against it. To Francis' surprise his old high school buddies were there to wish him a warm farewell.

"There he is! Where'd you pack your elephant gun, Frankie?" ruddy cheeked Dave announced from his towering frame. Ron chimed in sweeping his charcoal bangs away from his eyes, "Why this fellow doesn't need a gun to hunt down the wild game in Africa, he'll just smile at them and the reflection of the sun will blind them into submission."

Without missing a beat as the other school chums laugh, Greg, with his stocky build gave Francis such a bear hug that if unexpected would've knocked the stuffing clean out of anyone else but Francis planted his feet firmly on the floor when he saw Greg coming and locked his arms down to his side while inhaling to avoid any broken ribs. "What in the world are you guys doing here?" Francis asked grinning from ear to ear. Dave spoke up, "We heard there's going to be trouble in River City..." "that's with a T, an R, and an O..." Greg followed suit, "and that spells TROUBLE," Ron said reminding him of the well known play they performed together in high school.

Francis led them into the sitting room and subconsciously took his collar off in a metaphorical kind of way and became Frankie from high school again. Before he could even get a chance to introduce Angela, she announced that she'd like nothing more than to hear stories about Frankie but she had an appointment to meet and said goodnight pulling the door closed behind her.

"So tomorrow's the big day, huh?" Greg affirmed.

"Yes, I can't believe it's already here," Francis said shaking his head.

"Do you remember when our French teacher, Miss...uh," Ron said sitting up attentively.

"Robbins, Miss Robbins, wow, she was something," Dave beamed with a big smile.

Greg interjected, "She wanted us to dress up like Frenchmen and the entire play was in a language we couldn't even understand."

"We were supposed to somehow figure out when to move here and do this there even though we didn't have a clue what anyone was saying," Francis recalled.

"Maybe we should've taken her class, huh? It was all in French," Greg kidded.

"It might have been worth it. When Miss Robbins spoke in that French accent, I'd always feel guilty like I was doing something wrong just by listening to her talk," Ron said turning red, "sorry about that, Father," Ron said remembering he's talking to a priest.

"No, no, that's okay, I'm just glad I don't have to learn a different language for this trip," Francis said seriously.

They continued to laugh and reminisce about their high school days remembering how Francis was always the life of the party – Prom King and everything; they voiced their concern about the parish and offered their show of support for him personally. Francis appreciated it and admitted he'd lost the fire he once had and hoped the trip would rekindle a spark. They were all raised Catholic men and today with families can appreciate how difficult it is to shepherd a flock especially in these times of mistrust with respect to religion in general. Francis didn't ask them any questions about where or if they even attended a church because he didn't want their relationship to be affected by his title. This was a breath of fresh air for a little while to just be one of the guys. As he started loosening up a little, he began to realize the heavy load he'd been carrying. He didn't know how heavy the burden was and how much it had adversely impacted his life until he felt this sense of relief, it was another indication that he'd been trying to go it alone without God in the equation and now he's paying the price of being crushed underneath the worrisome weight of his trials.

Dave remained behind after the other fellows said their goodbyes to tell Francis he's been praying for him and believes that God has something truly special in Africa for him. Dave leaned over with that solid frame and whispered in Francis' ear, "It's all going to hit you like a huge wave. I believe God's spirit is going to overtake you like a perfect storm and you'll never be the same again, Frankie." Francis was stunned for a moment and said, "Maybe so, Dave," not sure how to take the statement, he asked, "Where are you going to mass these days, Dave?"

"Faith Christian Assembly," Dave briskly answered.

"Oh, I didn't realize you..." Francis stumbled for words.

"Yes, I know it's a surprise. It was a surprise to my whole family. They really don't understand," Dave said with his eyes to the ground, "Listen Frankie, we've known each other since we were kids. I know you usually pray for everyone else but do you mind if I pray for you before you take your trip?" Never having been in this situation before Francis thought for a moment and felt humbled considering his current spiritually dry place and politely accepted his friend's offer.

"Dear Lord God, I place Frankie in Your hands as You protect him from any danger on his trip to Africa. I ask that Your Guardian Angels go ahead of him as he travels. Create a pillar of fire of protection around him that he may find Your continued perfect will for his life. I ask that nothing get in the way of Your revelation. I pray Your peace will flood Frankie's soul as he opens his heart and mind to greater heights of joy that I believe will fill him up with the Holy Spirit. Overflow his cup so he can bring Your glory home to his parish that is in such need of a fresh spark of life from You, Lord. I pray this in the Name of Jesus." Francis couldn't describe what he felt as Dave prayed but he became noticeably choked up as he bid his friend farewell with a hug. He shut the door, broke down for a moment and closed his eyes with his hand pressed hard against the door. "This is the way I used to feel about God, like He's right here with me." He felt a new anticipation in his spirit and a lightness he'd not known for many years. Maybe this is all just

sentimentality along with leaving Maggie behind combined with a sense of relief from being dismissed from daily parish life yet he so wants to believe Dave, that there's indeed something waiting for him in Africa. He thought hard knowing he's going to have trouble sleeping and wondered if he would see Maggie or not before he left and if the board encouraged her to keep her distance. To avoid causing her any problems he silently prayed and drifted off to sleep asking God to make a way for them to say goodbye possible.

Chapter Seven

The Kindness of a Stranger

Although the alarm clock was set for very early morning, Francis abruptly woke up shortly before it rang. He felt a brushing sensation against his cheek as he sat up. He recalled a dream he had, he saw himself lying down in a field of clover where deer were feeding. It was strange, they were only eating select areas of grass and leaving large patches untouched. He saw a fawn back away from him and realized she whispered something in his ear, her eyelashes brushed against his cheek. What an unusual sensation! He thought back for a moment and recalled she said, "greener pastures." Now what could that possibly mean? Somehow he knew it was important and turned on the bedside light. Scratching his head he had an unusual and conflicted feeling about the dream almost a sense of dread when he pictured the deer feeding in the background as the fawn spoke in his ear. Even though a dream is perfectly benign, it made him feel uncomfortable and out of sorts because intuitively his senses told him it was somehow very profound. He couldn't help but wonder if it was God speaking to him through this dream and thought of Father Patrick, hoping his insight could give meaning.

Awaiting departure on the runway, Francis looked one last time out of his window hoping to see Maggie there, he wasn't aware that her early morning duties caused her to run late. When the engines started, he saw her waving at the window near the gate but he's not sure if she could see him. He hoped for a formal goodbye and she hoped for a formal farewell, the difference being a short season or holding quite possibly a lifetime. As Francis and Father Patrick buckled in, the flight attendant handed Francis a note from Maggie,

I was praying for you early this morning and saw a vision of you with Jesus in a glen feeding a doe. Does that mean anything to you? It seemed like He was showing you how to feed the doe properly. Do they have deer in Africa? I thought you should know. I felt you should know. God bless you, dear Francis. I'll miss you.

From his window seat, Francis gave the note to Father P as the plane cruised down the runway and started its ascension into the sky. Now he had the calm chance to begin describing the unusual dream to Father Patrick, who said, "you mean like that?" pointing out the window from his seat in the middle to the ground below.

"Yes, the patches of grass looked like plowed and unplowed fields next to each other like a checkerboard design," Francis said as he stared out the window.

"I can tell you one thing for certain, I don't think that note from Sister Maggie is a coincidence. Any idea what this is all about? What this all means?" Father Patrick asked with an inquisitive tone.

"No, I was hoping you might," Francis said curiously with a questioning tone in his voice, his eyes continuing to stare out the window.

"It brings to mind the verse of the deer panting for the water..."

"So my soul panteth after thee," Francis finished.

"Your spiritual drought, maybe?" Father asked with a twinkle in his eye. "I find it interesting your feeling like you'll find spiritual refreshment in such an arid place as Africa. That is where the greener pastures are?"

"Maybe that's why so many of us have a hard time figuring out God's will, we just don't think the way He does," Francis speculated shifting his weight in his seat.

"Yes, His ways are certainly higher. Sometimes I think we try to manipulate our lives the same way a tailor makes a fine suit – just lay out a pattern and cut along the dotted line with complete confidence we'll end up with something we're willing to wear," Father P reasoned.

"Kind of like 'playing it safe'?" Francis inquired.

"Well if you're determined to be led by the Great Shepherd you're bound to follow the narrow path on pretty rocky ground, wouldn't you say?", Father P pondered accepting a Cola from the flight attendant.

"Absolutely, but as one sheep who has more than a few sore spots on the backside from being tapped by His staff, I can tell you I don't exactly look for adventure, if that's what you mean," Francis said smiling.

"Going to Africa is adventurous, wouldn't you say?" Father P asked without equivocation.

"Yeah, if you told me this little Italian boy would be flying across the world to the dark continent of Africa, I would not have believed you. You know before I was born my folks thought they might have a girl and wanted to honor God by naming the baby, Theresa. I don't know what just made me think about that."

Father P asked, "Named after St. Theresa? The saint of miracles?"

"I can't believe I never told you this story before. Back in 1954 my father had stomach problems, they thought it was cancer and the real concern was he might not make it. But the family prayed for a miracle," Francis reflected.

"What happened?" Father P nudged Francis with his elbow.

"He had surgery, they found an egg sized tumor and removed two thirds of his stomach. He survived it and it was a miracle," Francis continued, "so they approached granny Grace to get her blessing to name the baby, Theresa."

"I see," Father P contemplated.

"Of course in an Italian family you name your children after the parents. To their surprise they had a son and I was named after my mother's father instead." Francis sighed sentimentally.

"Do you somehow feel like you're going to Africa on behalf of your whole tribe?" Father P grinned like the Irishman that he was.

"Well, even though I wasn't named for Saint Francis, my birth was kind of like thanks to God. There's always been a sense that I've been blessed from the womb. I would never be on my way to Africa if my father had died prematurely. I can assure you I never thought the road from there to here would have taken so many twists and turns along the way", Francis looked over at Father P intently.

"You've been looking for a fitted suit, my friend," Father P tapped his fingers on Francis' cuff laughing.

"Maybe that's it. I guess we shouldn't be so detailed that we're not willing to take one off the rack," Francis said with a whimsical glance.

"It's funny, two guys in collars talking about what suit to wear. But I guess I'm not a dotted line kind of guy. If God had asked me if I wanted to know in advance how my life would unfold, I would have declined," Father P said soundly.

"Really, why?"

"Because my faith would decrease figuring out every equation ahead of time. What fun would there be in that?" Father P said half joking but with discernment.

"Maybe I'm just the kind of guy who likes to skip to the end of the book to see how it all turns out and sometimes I think if I knew the next step God has for me, I might be more enthused and obedient."

"Don't forget, Francis, the excitement isn't in seeing the next step, it's in your motive for taking it. Love gives you the strength to take the first step when you're tempted to stand still. Love for God and for His children will get you to where you need to be, even if it's on a dusty road in Africa, and I assure you the only book that matters already has a really good ending. Mind if I sit by the window? I get a little motion sickness."

As Francis switched seats with Father P he apologized to the older gray haired lady sitting in the aisle for bumping into her as he moved into the middle seat.

"Hi, Father," she said with a sweet smile.

"Hello, I'm Father Francis and this is Father Patrick," he nodded in Father P's direction.

"My name is Ethel Louise but you can call me Louise. I've never talked to a priest before. Do you usually travel in twos like the disciples did?" she asked as she pointed to the pair of them.

"I never thought about it quite that way but the journey is easier when you have a friend to pass the time with," Francis admitted.

"You know, Father, it's been a very hard week. My best friend who wound up living in Africa after traveling there died suddenly from a heart attack, I'm headed to her funeral," Louise said with sadness.

"I'm so sorry to hear that. Was she a life long friend?" Francis inquired.

"Yes," she paused and thought back over their lives, "As a matter of fact I led her to the Lord many years ago. She was like a sister to me but she's with Jesus now," then Louise said, mainly to comfort herself, "I used to be afraid of dying but I had a near death experience that changed all that and I've been living with a new sense of boldness ever since."

Then Francis started to doze off while still trying to continue their conversation, he was intrigued by Louise's story of a second chance and amazed by such a sense of intimacy in her voice. She spoke and childhood memories stirred in him, they came flooding through his mind, he remembered sitting in catechism asking countless questions to his teacher and in her frustration she told him to ask a theologian the answers to such penetrating questions. Talking with Louise reminded him of that sense of wonder about God that he seemed to have lost and she obviously lives by.

"You're very inquisitive about God," Francis said turning slightly in his seat toward her, not meaning to pry, he was just curious.

"I wasn't before the accident. I mean I always considered myself a Christian even when I wasn't really going to church. But I didn't realize until I saw Jesus face to face in Heaven as I was sprawled out in the street down here that this life is fleeting and there's no time to waste," Louise said intently with a passionate yet practiced delivery like she'd delivered her testimony a million times before.

"But most people live their entire lives without having that kind of experience," Francis contemplated. A tear of joy rolled down Louise's cheek as she told Francis how fortunate she is to feel so different now. Instead of Jesus being like Santa Claus or the tooth fairy, He's like a member of her own family. She described it to Francis as having been born all over again. Everything seemed new, exciting and fresh. The strange thing is the feeling has never left her since she awoke from her 71 day coma. Louise described that Holy Easter Sunday morning when she sat up in her hospital bed with what the nurses described as an ethereal radiating glow on her face and an aura surrounding her, not sure if possibly she had another condition needing treatment or some side effect of medication, they actually called a doctor in. As Louise's words floated from her lips to his ears like butterflies freed from their cocoon, Francis found himself saying a silent prayer under his breath, *"Lord, let whatever this woman has rekindle something in me."* To Francis, Louise's joyful tears were somehow making their way into his heart. He started to actually feel its hardness begin to soften. Suddenly memories from years ago when his father died surfaced back into his mind, he saw his father's lifeless body being carried out in a body bag at 3:00 a.m. while his mother could only helplessly look on. Long forgotten yet buried pain gave way as feelings of love overwhelmed him; the love and comfort of everyone at the funeral mass where he was expected to preside. At the time he hadn't allowed himself to begin the healing process because he had to stay strong for his family, then after the funeral with emptiness and lack of consolation, a moment of despair led Francis into a powerful depression and anxiety stole any sense of joy and peace from his life.

But now this happenstance encounter with a Protestant woman on a plane bound for Africa started a landslide of emotion and a healing he's absolutely sure was ordained by God. So many years of being a public person wearing a religious face did nothing but camouflage his real sense of loss and remorse, perpetually growing the seed of sorrow created by all of that and which desperately needed to be pruned out of him. Like the priest nurse he is, he knew enough to sit and let her words breathe life giving hope to his soul like a surgeon cutting out a cancer that had robbed him for so long. When this heavenly procedure was over, he recalled what his friend Dave said the night before the trip, "God's got something in Africa for you, Frankie." He also knew that Maggie's prayers had something to do with this breakthrough. The fact that he hadn't even set foot on the land of his destination gave him pause to marvel at what else God might have in store for him.

Chapter Eight

Africa, at Last

Father Patrick and Father Francis stared in silence as the magnificent hues in the sky displayed all of the colors of the rainbow as day turned into night over the vast ocean when one time zone gracefully turned into another by the Creator of all. There was something peaceful and calming flying in the night but there was also something eerie and ominous in the respect that a night sky is measured by the stars which prevent the reality of infinity from overwhelming you. This label seemed somewhat apropos as they traveled into the darkness toward what some would call the dark continent of Africa. As priests they understood the spiritual implications of a nation steeped in voodoo and witchcraft, often preventing those suffering with affliction from gaining a leg up. God, the Father of all desperately wants to bless Africa where it is hurting the most and Francis felt like he was being led to investigate it.

He's excited and anticipating the reunion with their friends, a passionate medical missionary couple named Libby and Dr. Frankie Valequez, who are a living dedication to a mission of mercy. The connection made with these kinds of folks who live to relieve the suffering of a continent plagued with misery is a common bond giving hope, when all work together to reach one long slow milestone after another on the way to making a difference. Coming from the order of priests who are nurses, Francis understands what it means to aid the sick and suffering but he didn't realize then that the scope of God's plan would bring him to an entire new level of mercy by seeing it first hand.

After finishing his meal, Francis leaned back, closed his eyes and tried to answer what Maggie's vision and his dream meant. He quietly asked the Lord to reveal to him if they are connected, how they affect each other and what did the message mean? Was it from God? It would be easy to dismiss his dream as a mere aberration caused by fatigue or that the excitement of the trip caused overstimulation of his imagination but there's no denying Maggie's confirming vision. Francis strongly sensed in his spirit that there is real meaning in it all and it would all be revealed to him in God's time.

They finally arrived in Africa and according to Angela's agenda, Brother Isaac, an African born religious from a village church was to be their guide. He waited for them to deplane, holding up a sign so they would find him. He introduced himself and apologized to them that Libby and Frankie were unavailable to greet them, they were called away on mission business and would catch up with them later. Brother Isaac thought it best to settle them in first and then show them the surrounding villages. Francis felt an immediate kinship with Brother Isaac upon meeting him as the Apostle Paul did who had so many amazing journeys, who embraced other steadfast believers tending to the physical and spiritual needs of their communities.

As they drove, Francis couldn't help but notice the throngs of older women and men walking along the roadside dressed in beautiful bright colored clothing, the bold reds and yellows of the men's vests and the women's dresses dramatically came to life against the dark color of their skin.

"Where are they going?" Father Patrick asked. With a rich heavy accent Brother Isaac answered, "They are going to funerals right now; you'll notice it's mostly the older ones. The younger generation is whom they are burying. These folks are mourning the dead; they have come through the scourge of AIDS only to bury their own children." Both priests remained silent in the face of this revelation because they just didn't know what to say in response. Francis felt a lump in his throat as he held back tears and turned his head away, he peered out of the window of the car to keep his composure. He could see the compassion on Father P's face and knew that his heart was breaking, too.

In that moment of deafening silence something began to stir in Francis' spirit, but breaking the silence, Brother Isaac said, "That's only half of it, because of the volume of people and the congestion, funeral services are allocated to separate time slots for burial. So these tent gazebos that are here right now will be moved to a different venue for another stream of people who will attend funerals this afternoon. Eighty to one hundred people will be buried in services today in just this one graveyard." Francis began to imagine the graveyards in all of the communities across Africa and for a moment thought he was having a panic attack because he couldn't catch his breath. His mind was unwilling to wrap itself around what Brother Isaac was telling them. He said it in such a matter of fact way but with the greatest compassion. Francis knew Brother Isaac was telling the truth because of the way he spoke about it. He was relating a kind of familiarity of mere facts that had unfortunately become a daily occurrence. Thinking the exact same thing, Father Patrick leaned over and said to Father Francis, "I guess this very plague of loss makes burying so many at one time a normal but not casual event." As they got out of the car, Francis regained his composure and asked Brother Isaac a question, "Why are some of them carrying sod?"

Brother Isaac paused for a moment and said, "They actually chip the surface of the grass and bring clumps over to the grave when the service is done and place it on top of the grave as a way of saying that the issue is done now, it's over."

Father P said softly, "It's almost like tucking them in bed somehow."

"For a very long sleep," Brother Isaac added.

"Maybe not for those we can reach with the Gospel. They can know God and see the Lord face to face when this life ends." Then Brother Isaac was heard reciting A Psalm of David, Psalm 102 under his breath, "For He knows our frame and remembers that we are dust. As for a man, his days are like grass; he flourishes like a flower of the field; for the wind passes over and it is gone, and its place knows it no more."

Father P continued, "But the steadfast love of the Lord is from everlasting to everlasting upon those who fear him and his righteousness to children's children, to those who keep his covenant and remember to do his commandments."

"That's the blessing that breaks the curse of this generational plague," Father Francis chimed in.

"Do you not know Matthew 27:52?" asked Brother Isaac. Cheerfulness lifted their spirits as they listened to Isaac's words and Father P began to do an Irishman's jig swinging arm in arm with great joy. "And the tombs were also opened, and many bodies of the saints who had fallen asleep were raised and coming out of the tombs after His resurrection they went into the holy city and appeared to many." All of a sudden Father Francis burst into laughter, "My dream! The deer in my dream! What I saw in the field were graves! Deer were eating the grass on the graves as if to say, uncover these graves, it's not over! It's not done with." The three stood around the graveyard with silly grins hugging each other, trying not to look conspicuous with their delightful demeanors from feeling God's presence so strongly. It was becoming more clear, the reason behind the mystery for their visit. The trip had just begun and the Lord had much more in store for Francis who crossed the vast ocean to answer the call that He placed in his heart, answering back, "Send me, Lord, here I am, send me."

Chapter Nine

Samuel and Salvation

Francis had somewhat of a reputation for his immense smile and people's responses to it were a familiar behavior. When he and Father Patrick were shown their modest accommodations, he sensed the stares and persistent grins were launched by a renewed feeling of hope in such a hopeless setting. Father Patrick pointed out the sound of children playing, "This sound is the same no matter where you come from. It is something I've noticed after natural disasters; when the dust clears children occupy themselves with play, aside from their grim surroundings; you might never know that their lives were so recently devastated. The adults on the other hand have a more difficult time coping with the losses especially because of their sense of responsibility for the children." Certainly the graveyard was not the appropriate place for Francis to share his God-given gift of blessing someone with a smile. But he felt the need to lift the tired spirits of those suffering from the deadly plague of AIDS which never rests or gives one day of relief from the prompting of its toll.

As Brother Isaac explained the particulars of their quarters to Father Patrick, Francis was sidetracked by personally ministering to a young girl whose leg had been amputated either from disease or possibly an accident. Father Patrick noticed he'd lost his companion for the moment and reflected on the Lord never growing tired of seeing a man or woman of God attending to one of His children. Is there a more personal way to show someone you care than kneeling down and looking through the window of their soul and giving them the undivided attention that says you care? With all the technological progress that makes getting somewhere easier such as organized strategic plans to distribute needed goods, nothing can replace the simple touch and tender sound in the voice of someone like Father Francis, or Francis, who lives to share each moment of ministering to Jesus, the son of God within, by meeting the needs of those He loves so very much. It is indeed a beautiful sight and always a reminder to all Christians that a way must be found to do more. As for Francis and Father Patrick, they believe that God, the giver of life who created and watches over the cattle on a thousand hills can do all things if His servants are simply willing to obey.

When Francis finished speaking with the child, he came in and shared that cancer had taken her leg. With a questioning look the girl wanted to know what kind of God would do such a thing.

"It's not an unreasonable question," Brother Isaac said.

Francis responded, "It's hard enough for an adult much less a child to know the answer to such a difficult question."

With passion in his voice, Father Patrick responded, "It would be easy to just explain that this world is not our home and we're merely sojourners in this life. I understand why people lay blame at God's feet because He's so all knowing and powerful yet He gave us free will as an exercise to demonstrate His sovereignty. He's not threatened by our questions. Theologically speaking it's more easily explained and understood by recognizing our fallen world due to original sin perpetrated against God in the Garden of Eden where all humankind partook in the sinful nature passed down from one generation to the next." Francis interjected, "For example, you don't have to teach these little ones to lie, sin is a part of fallen nature since birth."

Brother Isaac asked in response, "Yes, and are we not made in God's image?"

Francis thought a moment and reasoned, "Yes, but our images are corrupted by sin and only God's love through the blood of Jesus can remove the curse of its detrimental affects bringing new life and restoration to a fallen and incomplete world. But it's hard to explain such things to someone who is in the midst of their suffering."

Father Patrick agreed shaking his head, "That's true, only a personal relationship with Jesus can heal the spirit, relieve the flesh and satisfy the soul to the big questions of life. So how did you answer the girl's question, Father Francis?"

"The only way I know how. I answered her with God's love, that God is love; I told her that when Jesus died on the cross He understood her suffering. Through sharing her pain with the Lord through prayer, she will know that God is for her not against her. Jesus died so she may live forever with God in Paradise and overcome anything that happens in life."

"That must explain the smile on her face after you spoke to her," Father P said delicately. Brother Isaac spoke up, "I wish that was the last sad story you'll listen to here but there are so many children left homeless and hopeless because their parents perished from the plague of HIV/AIDS."

Father Francis responded softly saying, "We're here to bring them hope."

Brother Isaac encouraged them that a good night's sleep would refresh them. After evening prayers, Father Patrick and Father Francis strolled about greeting many townsfolk. Later they reflected on the day's events as they prepared their hearts for what tomorrow will bring. As they walked by the village hospital, Francis recalled Brother Isaac say he led a hospitalized man named Samuel to the Lord recently. They decided to visit the hospital to pray with the sick. As Father Patrick made his way from one bed to another greeting each patient with a pleasant smile, Francis inquired about Samuel who was evidently suffering from pancreatic cancer complicated by AIDS. Unfortunately he'd fallen into a coma, but Francis believed the man could hear him regardless so he prayed over him and spoke to him about the things of God and how much the Lord truly loves and cherishes him. Overhearing Francis, the man in the next bed identified himself as Samuel's neighbor, who is also dying of AIDS.

"Do you know my friend?" he inquired using the best English he knew.

Francis told him this is his first day in Africa, that he's here on a mission trip. "Then how is it you know so many things about Samuel and that he understands fluent English?" In conversation he found out that what he'd been saying to this man's comatose friend were things that only those close to him could know. Francis felt compelled to ask this man if he knew Jesus and after conversing for a time with him, was given the grace to lead him in prayers of salvation. It was clear that God had stirred something in this man's heart when he first cried out to Jesus upon hearing his own medical prognosis.

They left the hospital and Father Patrick was prayerful while Francis was on cloud nine because another life had been snatched from the jaws of hell and delivered into the Kingdom of God. As the two men shared, they praised God and thanked Him for His everlasting mercy and the belief that many will be eased of their suffering and many afflictions that evening.

After retiring for the night, Francis woke up abruptly at 4:00 a.m. with a heavy desire in his heart to pray for Samuel who, to Francis' understanding was still in a coma. He felt lighter when he finished praying and praised God then drifted back to sleep. In the morning the news arrived that Samuel passed away early in the morning around the same time Francis prayed for him. Francis knew in his spirit that Samuel entered into God's glory when he praised God for hearing his prayers. Did Samuel come by and awaken him on his upward journey to Heaven? The line between life and death and Heaven and Earth is so thin. Samuel is with the Lord now.

Chapter Ten

Starfish on the Sea Shore

The sun is already hot as Father Patrick arose and washed away the remnant of yesterday's toil and sweat after he traveled thousands of miles to reach a new reality in a world so indescribably filled with human suffering and agony. Outside dust spools were swirling like little tornadoes dancing with one another and dying back down quickly as people walked by without even noticing these little wonders. The dirt filled twisters set a tone as Father P started his day off professing there are noticeable miracles around you if you're willing to pay attention. Father P thought about the patients at the hospital and prepared to join Francis in celebrating the miracle of Samuel's new deliverance from the arid African plains into the bosom of a Heavenly Father whose fertile green pastures provide unending delight. He knows that even in a desert, God placed an oasis of wonder yet Father P is looking toward the remainder of the day to see how it unfolds. After inquiring to the whereabouts of Father Francis, he's told he's gone to help a family living 16 miles due north. Evidently the mother is having difficulty giving birth and Francis, who's delivered many babies, offered his assistance. That was over three hours ago, it's probably too soon to be concerned but Father P is ready to be taken to the family's home to help in case of an emergency. Chuckling to himself, he remembered one of Francis' nursing stories about a similar situation when he was chased off at gunpoint by the husband of woman who was evidently expecting a midwife *not* a male nurse.

While traveling the bumpy road to the family's hut, the up and down motion is making him feel like a can of soda that's ready to explode, Father Patrick reflected back to what he'd once heard and is now experiencing first hand regarding the poor conditions of the roads which make travel a difficult and uncomfortable journey for anyone traveling on them and that the development of an interstate highway system in Africa would be the single most life-saving project anyone could undertake since life saving materials would get to their destinations on time. Fortunately the feeling subsided and he wondered how Father Francis was dealing with the fact that there are no real modern conveniences to speak of but having a background in nursing, they always carried supplies to provide basic medical attention whenever necessary.

The guide's young son pointed to a pride of lions lying under some trees as their tails flicked flies, their large tongues dangled down panting as the noon day sun approached its predestined perch. The driver assured Father P that they fed the night before and there's no need for concern. Instead as they approached the area, a roadblock prevented them from going any further. A young boy had been mauled by a female lion. The local authorities directed everyone to stay inside the stopped vehicle until everything was formally examined. Father P explained that he's with the church and has a medical background. The guard motioned for them to follow and hurried the men to a building standing alone with other vehicles parked around it. Once inside Father P sensed the level of stress and caught a glimpse of Father Francis leaning over the young boy stitching up a wound in his shoulder. Since Francis had been suturing for quite a while,

Father P offered to take over, it looked as though there were over one hundred stitches.

"Here, let me take over and give you a rest," Father P said with an expression of amazement on his face that this injured boy hasn't bled to death already.

"Someone saw the attack, that's the reason he'll make it. Whoever that was immediately applied pressure and kept the bleeding under control," Francis said with a sense of relief.

"I thought you were delivering a baby," Father P inquired as he pressed the next piece of flesh to be sewn together.

"Been there, done that," Francis smirked while taking a deep breath and released it. When the boy was stable they transferred him to the van and began driving to the hospital, they found out then from Brother Isaac that there was a guardian angel they had not known about. Isaac told them, "A stranger fended off the lioness after her attack and prevented her from killing the boy and directed the attention to himself instead. Then afterward no one could find the man."

"A complete stranger?" Father Patrick inquired. Brother Isaac nodded affirmatively as Francis looked in Father P's direction wondering if he's thinking the same thing he was but Brother Isaac beat them both to the punch when he said, "Maybe it was an angel."

"Maybe so, but wouldn't it be nice to think it was just someone willing to risk his own life for someone else's child?" Francis asked aloud.

"Yes," Father P said in agreement, "that sounds even better." They were almost to the hospital when the moaning boy began to wake while Francis tried to keep him from moving so the stitches wouldn't break open.

The young boy was admitted to the hospital and everyone there talked about the curious foreigners who saved the boy and brought him in. Libby and Frankie were already there and greeted them with smiling faces and in conversation began to describe their periodic journeys into the wilderness as matters of life and death because so many children are often left without medical attention once the adult population dies off in their small villages; they don't receive the attention necessary to preserve any basic level of health. Libby and Frankie travel close to 200 miles away to treat the children and bring as many as possible of the critical cases back to the hospital. Francis inquired with a compassionate voice, "What are the means to getting them back home once they're treated here?"

Frankie's wife, Libby answered with an experienced tone, "There really isn't much family left to return them to. Many are placed in orphanages and as supplies become available the others are treated for the AIDS they inherited from their mothers who've since passed away from the disease." As they shared, Francis recalled seeing so many fresh graves by the roadside and the overwhelming feeling of helplessness returned to him. This reflection was abruptly interrupted by the following staggering statistics, "Around the world thirty three million people are estimated to be infected with AIDS. Ten percent of this number is infected in one year alone," Frankie said as he took a deep breath. Libby continued, "In Africa alone there are 22 million infected with two thirds living in the Sub-Saharan areas. One in five die from causes related to AIDS. Life expectancy is less than 40 years old." The countless numbers of graves Francis tried to calculate in his head on the day they arrived and the grief of the townspeople now started to make sense as the face of AIDS came into clearer focus. Such devastating statistics like this made his stomach tighten. Father Patrick inquired, "How do you keep yourselves from becoming overwhelmed by such numbers?" Frankie wore a steely determined expression on

Chapter Eleven

A Needle Stick and Greener Pastures Away

In Africa, dust covers everything, it is really a challenge to adapt to the hot climate in such an arid part of the world. When Francis stepped outside and greeted the new day, it was already quite warm and his throat was dry from breathing in the night air. He took a drink from his water bottle and saw the sun sparkling through it, he thought of how dry his soul had become. In the same way that some have described Africa as a god forsaken place, he is made aware now of the depression that had stolen joy from his soul over the years like a dried up well; his parishioners also went thirsty as they continued to drop their buckets of hope into his well which should have brought them refreshment but left them parched instead.

Brother Isaac greeted Francis at the hospital and announced that Father Patrick was there with Frank and Libby who were attending to the sick. They have already introduced Mrs. Korobo to Father P, the RN who is affiliated with an organization that provides permanent traveling nurses to the region; she's the one they spoke of who takes care of many AIDS patients. As Francis swung the hospital door open, his eye caught a glimpse of a very dark-skinned slender woman with gray patches in her hair. He sensed this was Mrs. Korobo, he watched as she attended to the AIDS stricken patients with such great care, moving her hands over and across their sick body like tuning a fine piano, keenly listening and feeling for the reverberation of each vibration as the ailing body would respond back to her touch. This woman was obviously gifted by God, she is like a concert pianist who is finding the right balance, the right sensitivity, knowing exactly each note and how best to inspire the music of the spheres of the celestial body within, she leaned over each one as she examined them with a keen eye trained to detect even the smallest change in their symptoms. The expression on their faces showed a sense of relief from her touch filled with God's healing power. As she lifted her eyes from her work, she smiled at Francis as if to say *welcome to the front lines, Father*.

Libby, looped her arm through Francis' and said, "That's Mrs. Korobo, she's been up all night with a dying AIDS patient, I haven't been able to coerce her into getting any rest."

"She smiled at me like she knows me," Francis responded.

"I've been telling her all about your trip. She's anxious to meet you," Libby asserted.

"Just by watching her in action, you can tell she's born to do this," Francis said with amazement.

Libby's husband, Frankie, stepped through the doorway and interjected, "You may not be aware of it but Mrs. Korobo's best friend died of AIDS last night."

Francis asked Libby, "The AIDS patient she was attending to?"

Libby sadly shook her head yes and left them to convince Mrs. Korobo it's time to be relieved of her duty. Then Mrs. Korobo came over and introduced herself with a strong handshake apologizing for her haggard appearance. Francis offered his assistance and she gave him rubber gloves and asked him to give a shot to one of the patients. When he finished injecting, Mrs. Korobo asked him if he'd like to get something to eat. As they shared a meal she began to answer the questions Francis had regarding the blight of AIDS on the community.

"I've noticed a number of pregnant women," Francis declared solemnly.

"Yes, they have AIDS. About 18% of women in Botswana for instance, aged 15 – 19 are infected with HIV," Mrs. Korobo said with a noticeable tremor in her hand, he refocused his eyes away and before he could mention the tremor she interrupted him by commenting she's just tired. Mrs. Korobo continued by saying that they counsel and treat pregnant women to decrease the mother to child transmission of the disease and in the same way a pregnant mother needs proper prenatal nutrition, AIDS patients benefit from proper nutrition. In the case of an AIDS patient, treatment won't be as effective without relatively good health from a steady diet. "I see, their bodies can't handle the medication alone, unfortunately that makes sense," Francis said nodding his head up and down to acknowledge his understanding. "Yes, and all of the drugs in the world have very little chance of extending their lives. Especially because you can't get dying patients to take the medication after they've seen how sick their family members were from the adverse side effects inflamed by the malnutrition that suppresses the immune system. Even if there's enough so called "food" filling their stomachs with no nutritional value, this improper diet undermines the medicinal effects of the drugs."

As Mrs. Korobo continued with one statistic after another, Francis felt the familiar pit in the bottom of his stomach tighten reminding him of when he first arrived here after seeing one grave after another and the funeral processions conclude only to begin again. His heart filled with sadness as her eyes filled with tears when she described her 38 year old best friend suffering with AIDS take her last breath the night before, in her care, this dedicated nurse, her best friend.

Francis rubbed his hands together and contemplated what he's just learned. He came face to face with the grim reality check of the fear associated with this deadly disease because now he must keep to himself the fact that he stuck himself with the needle he'd used on one of the AIDS patients. He was listening so intensely to Mrs. Korobo and not paying attention when he put the syringe with an uncapped needle into a Sharps container which pierced the plastic and went through to the other side sticking the index finger of his left hand, the hand he was using to steady the container. He felt stupid and afraid. Fortunately no one had noticed him breaking out into a sweat due to anxiety of what this could mean but also the day was heating up so quickly and without a breeze the temperature was stifling hot. Is it possible that he came to Africa only to be infected by the very disease he wants to defeat? "Oh, no, not that! I'll take this secret to the grave with me," he thought to himself, "but I won't deal with it right now, I can't deal with it right now."

Over the next couple of days as they minister to the sick, he sought God privately in prayer and struggled with the incident again and again in his mind. The possibility of contracting the HIV virus caused Francis to reflect upon his life, his calling, even Maggie with a different perspective. Even the slightest risk of the loss of his health and maybe even his life made him refocus his attention from selfish matters to those of immediate concern. Suddenly finding a way to help those afflicted with AIDS, so far from his home, a world away, seemed even more urgent now. It was in those moments which gave him pause, he realized a new awakening in his soul fueled by gratitude as he stood where he was in the midst of poverty upon suffering and death and wanted even more to think outside of himself and reach out to others, he knew deep down inside how great his life really had been because of where he was born and lived, everything meant so much, he hadn't struggled as these here have, ever. He knew many AIDS patients in America through his work as a nurse and in the community of his parish but there are governmental programs and the deep pockets of wealthy citizens giving the opportunity for treatment and can't be compared to what is not even closely available in Africa, not to mention the additional hurtle of malnutrition blocking the way for effective treatment. "What can be done?" he blurted out. Francis didn't realize he shouted out loud until Mrs. Korobo answered his question, "What can be done? Is that what you need to know, Father?"

"Yes," Francis looked dazed for a moment, "How can I help you?"

"We need liquid nutrition, Father! It bolsters the immune system giving theAIDS patient somewhat of a fighting chance to live with the disease."

"Liquid nutrition, you mean in those little cans?"

"Yes, you see, increase 'resting energy expenditure' is the secret in persons living with HIV or AIDS, if they don't burn up as many calories, even sitting still, and keep their weight up, they have a fighting chance," Mrs. Korobo's eyes blazed with a fire built on a commitment to end this terminal suffering and turn it into a chronic illness as it is in the United States.

Francis was eager to share this new information from Mrs. Korobo with Father Patrick and to remind him of the mysterious dream of the appearance of the fawn saying the words *greener pastures* to him. With enthusiasm, Francis shared what he's learned with Father P, Frank, Libby and Brother Isaac, who humbly expressed his sincere gratitude to God for sending his brothers from across the sea bringing passionate hope to his fellow Africans who are suffering, helpless and hopeless at the hands of a disease which currently offers no chance of survival.

Francis immediately calculated the time difference between there and the United States in order to call Angela, he believed she would help him reach Maggie. She needed to know the importance of the conversation and connection to his dream especially in light of the note she wrote to him of her vision.

"Angela, greener pastures aren't *in* Africa, we must bring the nutrition of greener pastures *to* Africa through small cans of liquid nutrition," Francis compassionately exclaimed forgetting that he's talking to Angela, not Maggie. "Father Francis, slow down! What are you talking about?" Francis forgot she didn't know about his dream, he briefly described it to her then asked, "Can you get a message to Sister Maggie for me?"

"I suppose so, yes," Angela said cautiously.

"Tell her she's right on. Tell her I had a dream about a fawn that spoke the words greener pastures in my ear. It's about taking the greener pastures to the AIDS patients through liquid nutrition," Francis asserted.

"Father," Angela said, "I'm writing this all down but some other words are flooding into my mind."

"What? Tell me."

"You need an organization, a foundation, to do this. It should be called FAWN, standing for – Fighting AIDS With Nutrition." A noticeable silence pierced the airwaves for a moment, it was as if everything had stopped at once.

"Perfect! Yes! That's it! God is doing this, Angela, He has a plan, He's working through us."

After his call to Angela, Francis couldn't contain his enthusiasm as he shared with everyone what Angela said about the foundation and its name to provide liquid nutrition to Africa. He knew God answered his and Maggie's prayers for guidance. He was so overwhelmed, the burning of the new passion in his belly had totally replaced the feeling of uneasiness about the needle stick. One way or another he is now a part of the landscape of the big picture of AIDS and he's determined his part is to make a significant difference. Even with the mere glimpse of this idea called FAWN, Francis was ready to turn in his sand shovel for a bulldozer to clear starfish by the thousands into the life giving waters of God's healing love.

Chapter Twelve

Angela Visits Sister Maggie

Angela decided she would deliver Father Francis' message to Sister Maggie in person. She couldn't wait to see the surprised look on Sister Maggie's face when she arrives at the convent. She called ahead for the Mother Superior's permisson and forgiveness for such short notice to visit. The Mother Superior was very happy to hear that she would be visiting and told her that Sister Maggie had been a little down in the dumps lately probably from homesickness.

Angela was so wrapped up in her own dismay about Father Francis and Sister Maggie both leaving the area at the same time that it hadn't completely occurred to her that they also must really miss one another. Losing the two at the same time had been very difficult for her. She remembered the sound of Father Francis' voice on the phone, not hiding the tenderness in his voice when he spoke Sister Maggie's name. Angela knows they love each other very much, while growing up she daydreamed about what it might have been like if they'd been a real biological family. In her fantasy, Father Francis wasn't a priest but a minister instead doing the Lord's work, Sister Maggie at his side as the perfect pastor's wife and she, the dutiful daughter. Angela, of course, had no real experience or knowledge of what it meant to be a P.K., or a preacher's kid. Although chairing the church board gave her insight of what it would be like to fall under the pressure of living in a fish bowl with expectations unrealistically set high by a church community toward a clergy family but Angela liked to think it would have been a perfect scenario. She was raised by a single mother and could only imagine what it would be like to be part of a 'whole' family. She had no regrets because God provided a loving and secure environment for her when growing up through her extended spiritual family. As far as she was concerned, she couldn't love Father Fancis or Sister Maggie more if they'd been her own parents. Her daydreaming was a compliment of how much she cared for them.

The look on Sister Maggie's face when she saw Angela was priceless as the young woman flew into her arms, "I know you haven't been gone very long, but I couldn't help but use Father Francis' call as an excuse to come and see you!"

"Father Francis called? When? When did he call you, Angela?" Sister Maggie pressed on. "Last night. He wanted you to know he dreamt that a fawn was speaking into his ear and spoke the words *greener pastures*. He didn't know what it meant until he found out that AIDS patients need liquid nutrition on a regular basis for their medicine to work effectively. Then he said we should bring greener pastures to Africa. He also said that in the dream the deer were eating what looked like plots in a field but they were really eating the grass off of the graves as if to say, it's not over – their fight for their lives, that is. Maggie, he was overcome by the site of so many graves from the deaths of the AIDS victims. It grieved his spirit." Angela spilled her heart out.

"Did he tell you I saw Jesus teaching him how to feed a deer in my dream?" Sister Maggie inquired enthusiastically. "Yes," Angela quietly said, "and I told him the organization he's going to start should be called FAWN – Fighting Aids

With Nutrition. Isn't that exciting?" After having prayed so hard, Sister Maggie began to beam and glow as if she was expecting a spiritual birth. She knows this is God's plan for Father Francis and can't help but wonder how or if she will fit into the equation. Why would God have shown her the vision if He hadn't meant for her to participate in Father Francis' new beginning? She's been so blue because of missing everyone but for Angela's sake she decided to perk up and enjoy their visit. Mother Superior asked the other nuns to cover Sister Maggie's responsibilities so she could enjoy extra time with Angela. This is not at all uncommon because sometimes when young women who are confused or need counseling visit the convent, the nuns then share duties in order for another to give her undivided attention to the one in crisis that had shown up on their doorstep.

Angela saw first hand during her visit that a convent is like stepping back into a simpler time when the daily duties of life are taught as part of the spiritual walk. The monotony of such chores gave one time to reflect upon their relationship with God. This is contrary to the modern world where attention is given to finding a way to get these responsibilities down to a minimum through technology leaving more time for leisure. But when life circles around only work and leisure there often isn't enough time for reflection, prayer or for communing with God. In the convent, God is not only found in the mass but in the silent moments while washing dishes or scrubbing floors. "I envy you, Sister," Angela reflected. "Just because we're in a convent, doesn't mean you have to call me sister you know," she teased. "I suppose. My life's so busy with so many things. I can't keep track of it all. It must be nice to go away and get a chance to just breathe," Angela said thoughtfully. "It is. I've enjoyed the quiet. I have to confess though, I'm a little different than most nuns who dedicate themselves entirely to focusing on God. My mind has a tendency to wander," Maggie admitted. "To Father Francis, you mean?"

Angela asked attentively. "Maybe, and to you, too and home," Sister Maggie said deflecting Angela's comment.

"It's strange you being here with Father Francis so far away in Africa," Angela said romanticizing.

"I know it all sounds very exotic to a young woman like yourself, it's not as if Father Francis is on a safari," Sister Maggie reminded Angela with an eyebrow in the air.

"Well, Father Francis would say he's on a soul safari," Angela speculated.

"Yes, that is something Francis would say," Sister Maggie choked up a little.

"You don't call Father Francis by his given name very often," Angela said with a question in her voice to elicit a response from Sister Maggie.

"I know but I can let my guard down a little when he's so far away. Who's going to know but you and God, and God already knows my heart. Right?" Maggie said.

"I can tell how much you care about Father Francis," Angela asserted.

"I suppose that means everyone else can, too," Maggie quipped.

"Not necessarily. I pay more attention when you two are together because you've both meant so much to me over the years. I don't think you realize what a difference you've really made in my life," Angela said with sincere appreciation and gratitude.

"You're like a daughter to me, if a nun can have a daughter,' Maggie laughed.

"I remember when you told me how things happened with you and Father Francis, the brief engagement and all,"Angela said.

"You mean the 24 hour engagement?" Maggie said as she smiled, "The call was too strong in Father Francis. I couldn't get in the way of what God wanted him to do," Maggie said intently.

"But it could have been different. Did you make the choice for him?" Angela inquired.

"Maybe but there's no point in thinking about that. It's important to believe that God has a plan for you and sometimes you have to put your personal desires aside to help fulfill God's plan," Maggie reasoned.

"It seems like a high price to pay, doesn't it?" Angela asked brushing her hair out of her eyes. "No, not really, when you look at how many people will be touched by what God's doing through Father Francis in Africa," Maggie said wtih assurance.

"But couldn't God have sent you together on a mission trip as a married couple?" Angela questioned. "You don't understand what drives Father Francis. Did you know when he was a boy, he never missed going to church? How many children do you know who are that enthusiastic about the faith at such a young age? Even in the middle of the week, he'd ride his bike to mass. He said he was there so often he wondered if other people thought he might want to be a priest. I think that embarrassed him a little," Maggie shared. "I didn't realize he felt so driven at such a young age," Angela confessed.

"Oh, he was. I would have loved to have been around him as a child. I'm sure to some it seemed odd but to others, even then, he was a role model," Maggie imagined.

The young boy was admitted to the hospital and everyone there talked about the curious foreigners who saved the boy and brought him in. Libby and Frankie were already there and greeted them with smiling faces and in conversation began to describe their periodic journeys into the wilderness as matters of life and death because so many children are often left without medical attention once the adult population dies off in their small villages; they don't receive the attention necessary to preserve any basic level of health. Libby and Frankie travel close to 200 miles away to treat the children and bring as many as possible of the critical cases back to the hospital. Francis inquired with a compassionate voice, "What are the means to getting them back home once they're treated here?"

Frankie's wife, Libby answered with an experienced tone, "There really isn't much family left to return them to. Many are placed in orphanages and as supplies become available the others are treated for the AIDS they inherited from their mothers who've since passed away from the disease." As they shared, Francis recalled seeing so many fresh graves by the roadside and the overwhelming feeling of helplessness returned to him. This reflection was abruptly interrupted by the following staggering statistics, "Around the world thirty three million people are estimated to be infected with AIDS. Ten percent of this number is infected in one year alone," Frankie said as he took a deep breath. Libby continued, "In Africa alone there are 22 million infected with two thirds living in the Sub-Saharan areas. One in five die from causes related to AIDS. Life expectancy is less than 40 years old." The countless numbers of graves Francis tried to calculate in his head on the day they arrived and the grief of the townspeople now started to make sense as the face of AIDS came into clearer focus. Such devastating statistics like this made his stomach tighten. Father Patrick inquired, "How do you keep yourselves from becoming overwhelmed by such numbers?" Frankie wore a steely determined expression on

AIDS, Love's Fight

Father P offered to take over, it looked as though there were over one hundred stitches.

"Here, let me take over and give you a rest," Father P said with an expression of amazement on his face that this injured boy hasn't bled to death already.

"Someone saw the attack, that's the reason he'll make it. Whoever that was immediately applied pressure and kept the bleeding under control," Francis said with a sense of relief.

"I thought you were delivering a baby," Father P inquired as he pressed the next piece of flesh to be sewn together.

"Been there, done that," Francis smirked while taking a deep breath and released it. When the boy was stable they transferred him to the van and began driving to the hospital, they found out then from Brother Isaac that there was a guardian angel they had not known about. Isaac told them, "A stranger fended off the lioness after her attack and prevented her from killing the boy and directed the attention to himself instead. Then afterward no one could find the man."

"A complete stranger?" Father Patrick inquired. Brother Isaac nodded affirmatively as Francis looked in Father P's direction wondering if he's thinking the same thing he was but Brother Isaac beat them both to the punch when he said, "Maybe it was an angel."

"Maybe so, but wouldn't it be nice to think it was just someone willing to risk his own life for someone else's child?" Francis asked aloud.

"Yes," Father P said in agreement, "that sounds even better." They were almost to the hospital when the moaning boy began to wake while Francis tried to keep him from moving so the stitches wouldn't break open.

"He didn't feel awkward at all," Angela said.

"Oh, I'm sure he did sometimes. He told me a funny story about how he'd go to mass every morning and then go pick up his buddy for school," Maggie said chuckling.

"So, what's funny about that?" Angela questioned.

"His buddy thought he was just coming from home. So when his friend called the house one morning and Francis wasn't around, Francis later came up with an excuse that he must have been in the shower or something and his father didn't know where he was. At the time I guess the idea of a teenager faithfully going to church every day wasn't exactly cool." Maggie laughed.

"Why? Is it cool now?" Angela smirked.

"I suppose not. Even though I think Jesus was the coolest person who ever lived. He didn't have any qualms about telling those who followed Him they'd also have to expect to be persecuted for their faith. But what's important about the story of Father Francis' journey is the fact that even though he might have been a little embarrassed nothing prevented him from doing what he felt was important," Maggie said intently.

"Yeah and look at Father Francis now, he walks around wearing a priest's collar as a reminder of what his life is dedicated to," Angela asserted.

"I believe as much as the Church has suffered from the sins of its leaders and followers alike that a call to holiness to one's belief shines forth to remind people that the God who died to pay for their sins is the same God who can help them face and overcome the sin that ravages their lives. That even though these past few years have been hard, Father Francis is a trailblazer in that area and always will be," Sister Maggie said nodding her head in affirmation.

As Angela concured with everything Sister Maggie shared with her, she wondered if they were tempted by sins of the flesh toward each other but she wouldn't dare ask that. Somewhat surprised by Maggie's mood she just smiled, she's never seen her so reflective and melancholy before. But Angela is not sure if it's a good thing or not. She's grateful that Sister Maggie has not forgotten Father Francis and like a schoolgirl, she's relieved that the two favorite people in her world haven't changed the way they feel about each other; she couldn't possibly handle her fantasy of them being a truly happy and content family together being shattered. The question is, when will they be together? Only God knows the answer and it remains to be seen whether the plains of Africa and the green hills that encircle the cloistered convent are too far apart to find a way for Father Francis and Sister Maggie to embrace once again.

Chapter Thirteen

The Temptress

Gasping for breath, Francis took out a handkerchief and covered his nose and mouth as a cloud of dust encircled him and Father Patrick fanned the air with his hat. They can't see what's caused all the commotion but when the dust cleared there were five vehicles parked in front of the hospital. There were two military vehicles, two decorated government transports and an ambulance. They saw attendants loading a patient and were surprised as a soldier came across the road and spoke to them, "You are the doctors who worked on the Governor's nephew who needed stitches from the attack of the lioness?" he questioned with authority. Father Patrick replied, "Yes, my friend, we attended to him. As you can see, we are also priests as well as nurses."

"Please come with me," he ordered as he motioned them toward one of the decorated vehicles.

"Where are we going?" Francis inquired.

"The Governor wishes to thank you properly for your service to his brother's son," the man professed.

Francis asked Brother Isaac to come along so they might have a better understanding of what's happening. Brother

Isaac spoke with the soldier and after a few minutes he announced it was okay to go with the soldier but to expect to be gone at least overnight.

"Then we'd better pack some things," Father P instructed.

"No need, everything will be provided," the soldier assured them.

Francis and Father P looked at each other in amazement and then proceeded to slide themselves into one of the long sedans that have decorative flags flying from each corner. Their part of the vehicle was sectioned off by what appeared to be bulletproof glass so they felt free to talk openly about this unexpected adventure. Just then, Father Patrick's cell phone rang. When he answered it, he heard the very calm and collected missionary voice of Libby on the other end. She instructed him not to worry. She and her husband believed this to be a divine appointment that could lead to wonderful inroads to heads of state for their cause. As Father Patrick put Francis on the phone, Frankie greeted him and began to run down a list of concerns. The first had to do with ministerial affairs in regard to removing roadblocks for the delivery of many goods to help the local communities fight disease and malnutrition. Next, the hurtles of protocol for gaining access to areas restricted from Christian evangelism due to political issues and or danger from infighting among warring religious and cultural factions. Francis was a little lost as he handed the phone back to Father Patrick. "I guess they think us Irish and Italian priests will get an audience wtih someone of influence, huh?" Father P said as his face flushed red from grinning. "I'm no politician, so God will have to put the words in my mouth," Francis squirmed. "He will, don't you worry about that. Just be who God made you to be and talk plainly. They know how to translate whatever you've got on your mind into the language required to get things done in their own government. The worse thing we can do is pretend to understand how things work," Father P said wtih persuasion.

"Well, I'll keep my ears open for opportunity with my prayers pointed toward Heaven but I'm not going to presume anything," Francis declared.

"That's wise. God will give us favor in the areas He wants us to have it in," Father Patrick assured him with a nod and a wink.

As the vehicles rolled into the government compound with its high gates and military decor, Francis couldn't help but think of the Old Testament prophets who were called before men of influence. He gulped hard as they stepped into the harsh sunshine, they were escorted to a large impressive room and instructed to wait there. Refreshments were provided and the two priests silently prayed for guidance. After what seemed like a long time, the large double doors swung open and a most beautiful woman glided into their presence. The gentleman who opened the door announced her as the sister of the Governor. She was sent to greet the foreigners because the leader was being detained by pressing business. The strikingly beautiful woman was tall and slender with the most perfect bone structure set off by exquisite eyes framed with the brilliant colors of a headdress that she balanced with delicate grace. Francis was amazed at God's creation of the delicacy of such human beauty and tilted his head down in acknowledgement as she greeted them. He was unaccustomed to being introduced to royalty and felt uncomfortable at that moment. Francis' self consciousness dissipated as Father Patrick took the woman's extended hand in his and seamlessly greeted her with a fatherly smile.

With a most charming accent, she asked them to be seated. For some reason she directed herself more toward Francis. She thanked them for saving the life of her nephew who was mauled by the lioness. "The female lion is the most ferocious," she said with a deep tenor voice as her eyes swept across the room to the doorman then affixed upon Francis. Just then he felt a shiver go up his spine. There was something very alluring about this woman that he couldn't pinpoint. He'd begun to feel self conscious once again as she seemed to stare deeply into his eyes. Momentarily he broke eye contact with her because of his discomfort with her imposing gaze. Even though he's wearing priestly garb, he felt completely exposed in this woman's presence as she continued to scrutinize him. Francis couldn't help but wonder if maybe her brother, the Governor, sent his sister into meetings with other heads of state to throw them off their game through intimidation.

"You have a most engaging smile; Father, is it?" She said with intention. "Uh, yes, sister. I mean, Father is correct. A man of the cloth, a priest that is to say," Francis was never so flustered in his life and was embarrassed at fumbling his words in front of Father Patrick. Father Patrick then played interference, "We are Catholic priests, recognized by the Vatican as emissaries of the faith in Christ Jesus, however, we are not on the Pope's business." Without even breaking eye contact with Francis, she responded with a quick lift in her step and turned in one swift motion toward the door. As she turned to leave, she told them they'll be escorted into the Governor's presence. Francis' stature noticeably relaxed as he took a deep breath and shook his head as he dabbed his forehead with a handkerchief. Both men simultaneously began to laugh out loud when the door finally closed and they were once again left alone. The echo of their laughter bounced off the walls of the large room.

"What was that?" Francis spouted.

"That was the devil's handmaiden, I think," Father P speculated.

"Why do I get all the attention?" Francis said with humility.

"Just lucky I guess," Father P said with a chuckle. "Didn't you know that black widow spiders like fresh meat when they sit on the side of their webs waiting for a likely prey?" Father P surmised.

"Come on, you're freaking me out. As if I don't already have the heebie-jeebies," Francis said rolling his eyes.

"I'm just having a little fun with you, my young friend. Before you let her attention go to your head, I'm pretty sure your collar had more to do with her attentiveness than anything else," Father P said giving insight to the younger priest.

"You're wearing a collar," Francis said reminding his mentor of his theory.

"Remember, I visited Africa many years ago. Believe me when I tell you, the vibes coming off this woman are spiritual in nature, and I use that term loosely," Father P stared straight ahead as if remembering.

"What kind of spiritualism? As in voodooism?" Francis asked.

"More than likely she believes if she can bewitch you, she'll gain power from your priestly station in this life, bringing you over to the dark side of the force, so to speak", Father P said with an eerie sound in his voice.

"Now come on! Are you kidding me?" Francis said feeling as if he's being toyed with.

"No actually, I'm not kidding about the underlying Satanism that runs through many of the teachings about evil supposedly being able to hijack power from good," Father Patrick said intently with all seriousness.

"Well, whatever it is, it makes me feel very uneasy," Francis openly admitted.

Father Patrick said, "Back in my day, we would have called for a deliverance."

Francis glanced at Father P expecting a cynical look on his face but instead found his demeanor to be completely serious. He started to contemplate what to expect next when a man entered the room informing them that the Governor wouldn't be able to meet with them today after all, then they were led down the hall to a wing of adjoining suites, and since they are a far distance away they must now stay overnight. They were asked not to leave their rooms, food would be sent up to them. Their accommodations were large and comfortable but they were quite disappointed in the news of this postponement. As Francis said his nightly prayers, his thoughts drifted to Maggie and he hoped she received his message from Angela. He felt sheepish about the encounter today, he's been around all kinds of women before but was still surprised by his reaction. He readily accepted Father Patrick's explanation of the situation but still felt a little unsettled. Then he heard a knock at the door.

"Come in!" he blurted out being lost in thought and somewhat caught off guard. The two doors flew open by a stainless steel cart covered with white linen. The Governor's sister announced, "Dinner is served, Father!" She darted the cart right over to Francis; he couldn't believe such a woman would actually serve guests. With one motion she tossed off the cover of a dish and swept up an African delicacy in one hand as Francis backed against the adjoining wall to Father Patrick's room. "Oh, Father Patrick?" Francis said in a high pitched voice as he banged his fist against the wall. "He has his own dinner, Father," she said perturbed by the intended interruption. She forcefully placed one palm on his chest, holding him firmly against the wall and shoved something unidentifiable into his mouth. Francis' eyes were as big as saucers. For a slim framed woman, she easily pinned him against the wall like a stuffed gazelle. He swallowed wtihout hesitation and began to silently pray for guidance. He didn't want to offend the Governor's sister especially before they've even had the opportunity to meet him but he wasn't exactly sure how to disarm this formidable seductress. Francis then said, "May I pray for you?" Just then this woman's beautiful eyes narrowed as she backed away and circled around the cart lifting another lid from one of the numerous selections. "Are you not hungry, Father?" she asked. "Francis stepped away from the wall and sat down in the chair across from the bed and said, "It seems to me that you're the one who's hungry."

"There are many exotic delicacies you've probably never tasted before?" she said expecting him to read between the lines, but he does not take the bait. "There is a biblical passage that says man cannot live by bread alone but by every word that comes from the mouth of God," Francis asserted. "Does that mean your God does not care about Africans who have no bread?" she sniped at him knowing very well corrupt governments are often responsible for the starvation of its people due to elitism. "The church is here to help," Francis responded sincerely. "Help? At what cost? There are strings attached to our kind of help. Is that not true?" she said continuing to investigate the cart's offerings. "I confess we desire to feed not only the stomach but the soul as well," Francis said carefully. "The heritage of Africa is our own. It is who we are," she proclaimed. "We have Christians on one side and Muslims on the other. We are in the middle being pulled apart but there is an Africa worth fighting for betwixt and between it all." "I agree. But those so called Christians and Muslims who steal, rape and kill in the name of Christ or Allah don't represent the hearts of the majority. The leader of our faith, Jesus Christ, teaches us to love everyone because all people are precious in His sight," Francis made direct eye contact intentionally. "We can help ourselves spiritually and every other way," she said contemptuously returning his stare. "If every Christian and Muslim left Africa, would it help?" he asked. "Yes, these demons have afflicted our people for generations," she said sorrowfully.

For the first time Francis saw a softness in her face and heard it in her voice. He asked her about the white magic that she believed would deliver her people from the affliction of the black magic. He reminded her that history tells a story of one African tribe enslaving another to gain power and prosperity at the others' expense. Francis revealed there are factions not just within her own people but all around the world, including America trying to take advantage of Africa's rich natural resources. Francis knows God has a plan and purpose for Africa, that she, as a continent of diverse countries can take her rightful place amongst other cultures healed from the generational curses of destruction. Africa can shine brightly to make a unique contribution to the blessed Earth God created.

Francis was relieved that the conversation shifted from a personal nature to a spiritual one. He also knew not to let his guard down. The dark art this woman takes part in is no laughing matter. Francis prepared for his bed after she left his room to retire for the night. He was astonished at the difference between the stir of emotion he felt upon meeting this exotic temptress and his honest feelings for Maggie so pure in contrast. To Francis it highlighted a vast chasm between the lust of the flesh the woman compelled and true beautiful trust between two loving servants of God that call themselves not only priest and nun but man and woman. He is grateful for women like Maggie who honorably reflect the image of the one true God.

Chapter Fourteen

Kidnapped!

After a restless night and a bedside breakfast, Francis and Father Patrick were visiting as voices were heard in the hall. Two soldiers appeared in the open doorway and announced their intention of whisking the two priests away to another part of the installation. After walking some distance inside the complex, they were escorted into a small but elegant room with a couch and two adjacent chairs sitting between two large pillars. Even before they could be seated, a distinguished man with graying temples dressed in opulent military gear walked in and greeted them. "Please, be seated. May I offer you something to drink? Coffee or perhaps tea?" the Governor asked briskly. "No, thank you. Breakfast was plenty," Father Patrick responded. "I apologize for not being able to greet you yesterday. Lately there have been many heated political issus that demand my attention," the Governor stated, rubbing his forehead, "I thank you for saving my brother's son from dying in a pool of his own blood. You have saved his life and I am in your debt."

"It is what we do, Governor. We are nurses as well as priests. Having heard the boy is your nephew, I was under the impression that he was your sister's son," Francis said.

"No. You have met my sister?" the Governor questioned intently.

"Yes, she..."

"Please let me apologize for anything she might have said to you. She is very dramatic and has no problem letting her mind be known to anyone who will engage her. Sometimes I think she spends too much time alone. Hopefully she did not offend you, "the Governor said as he motioned to one of the guards to pour him a cup of tea from the tea set on the small table next to his chair. Father Patrick responded, "No, no, I think Father Francis especially found your sister a very stimulating conversationalist." Francis tossed a glance at Father P as if to say thanks a lot, "Your sister is very passionate about Africa, Governor."

"Yes, I know and her heart is in the right place. I very much would like to utilize her enthusiasm but personally I find her theology a little suspect," the Governor said with surpising transparency. Francis was surprised at the Governor's use of the word theology considering his sister referred to herself as a spiritualist. As much as she put Francis on the alert, the Governor on the other hand gave off a very warm and compelling kindness in his demeanor, noticeable through the military ceremony of his position.

Suddenly an alarm sounded. The expression on the Governor's face went from benevolent to serious as if taking off one mask and putting on another. Before he could get to his feet, gunshots were heard in the corridor. The two guards shuffled the guests off into an adjoining room as the Governor told them they must change out of their priestly attire immediately quickly explaining that fundamentalist terrorist organizations were poised to overthrow the government. His own military had been compromised, inflitrated by extremists over the last six months. He didn't know who he could trust, he is especially worried about these two men being identified not only as Americans but religious authorities as well.

"Are you telling me they might kill us?" Father Patrick asked with no answer back it was quickly realized that was the fact.

As the two men quickly put on street clothes, Francis leaned over to Father P and said, "I'd be more worried about being held for ransom and tortured."

"Your friend could be correct, depending on their agenda, they may or may not want the kind of worldwide attention such a demand would bring. However, extremists don't always care about a particular result as much as standing on principle," the Governor said as the men were instructed to exit out an open window onto the searing hot rooftop.

Gunfire continued to blast as they dropped down into an open courtyard with bombs blasting nearby. As they rushed around a corner, half a dozen rebels shoved all three men down while machine gunfire shot down the two soldiers. Just as Francis responded to aid one of the fallen victims, a rebel pressed his firearm firmly into his neck, the hot barrel burned his skin. The men spoke quickly in their native tongue as the Governor tried to engage the men but to no avail. A truck pulled up and they were thrown head first into the back and tied hand and foot with a gag between their teeth. Francis noted drips of sweat rolling down the Governor's brow as it made its way through the sun scarred lines on his face from years of exposure to the harsh elements. His eyes were fixed and didn't show any signs of stress, only resolve. The governor was a man who fought many wars and carried himself as a warrior and wore it well. However leading men into battle and his responsibilities as a political figurehead were two different types of danger. In this part of the world, overthrow often resulted in making an example of the previous government officials. Francis noticed Father Patrick bowed his head in prayer and spoke under this breath, then

Francis observed something unexpected, he saw the Governor bow his head in prayer speaking in his native language and then he became the third strand in a cord of prayer asking God's will be to done in their hour of need.

Hours went by and the dust from the road was swirling into the back of the truck making it difficult enough to breathe but it was doubly hard due to the gags in their mouths. When the truck came to a stop, Father Patrick was thrown hard onto the floor of the vehicle. Francis knelt down to desperately try and help his friend up but Father P just laid there breathing rapidly. Francis then turned his body around and used his hands to pull the gag from Father Patrick's mouth so he could get some air. Without warning, the Governor and Francis were yanked from the back of the truck and blindfolded. As they were led off, one lone shot was heard, the sound sent a chill through Francis. He couldn't see anything and wasn't sure what happened. They were thrown into a cramped room with barred tiny windows that let some light in through the narrow openings along the very top edge of the ceiling. The guards untied them and removed the gags from their mouths. Where was Father Patrick? Why would they separate them? When the soldiers left, Francis asked the Governor, "Where is Father Patrick?" With a look of hesitation on his face, the Governor said, "We cannot be sure of anything right now."

"What was that shot I heard right after we got out of the truck?" Francis said with extreme concern in his voice. Just then a voice could be heard through the bars in the door, "It's a guard," the Governor said. "What's he saying?" demanded Francis. After pausing briefly in silence, he hesitantly answered, "I'm sorry, your friend has been executed," the Governor said sadly. Francis tried to catch his breath and put his head between his legs. He felt numbness cover his entire body as his mind tried to understand what his ears have just heard. Maybe the Governor misunderstood what the guard said. Maybe Father Patrick was shot but only wounded. It can't be true, that his faithful companion was brutally gunned down. Then a thought too painful to consider crossed Francis' mind, did they shoot Father Patrick because Francis removed his gag? Was that the offense that took his life? Was he responsible for Father Patrick's death because he helped him to breath?

Later that evening, Francis turned down the food that was slid underneath the door. His stomach was tied in knots and cramps at the very notion of food. He lost count of how many times he leaned over the small toilet in the corner of the room because he felt sick, but nothing would come up. No words were spoken between he and the Governor only quiet sobs of sorrow could be heard coming from Francis' cot. His mind raced but sleep eluded him even in spite of his exhaustion. Once Francis closed his eyes, he wasn't sure if he was dreaming or not. He saw a man sitting down on his haunches in the middle of a dungeon, with a stream of light coming through a small opening above that illuminated the top of his head and rolled down over his slight shoulders. This man's frame was emaciated as if starvation had taken its toll. His eyes were shadowed by the deep dark cavernous sockets which no light emanated from. His shoulders were slumped as his slender arms fell to his sides with his face peering upward. In his dream Francis asked, who is this man who appears to be on the edge of death? After a moment, he began to recognize the man despite his obvious depleted physical condition. "It's me," Francis said to himself looking at a surreal self portrait, "This is a prophetic vision of what God said my soul is beginning to look like, frail and faithless, frigid, fatigued, withered and worn."

The image was so startling that Francis physically shivered as if a cold breeze blew through the humid little structure where he found himself held captive. But his physical person was not what he was concerned with. His sights were set heavenward especially with the vibrant memory of Father Patrick still in his mind. He didn't want to die in the middle of the desert with the soul of the man from that unusual image he envisioned. Francis desparately desired to finish well. It was a moment of truth, your life flashes before your eyes when that moment of danger comes and in the twinkle of an eye, you are standing before God making an account of your life. Francis didn't want to just be wearing the gown of salvation but desired the robe of righteousness attributed to a race well run for Christ when his time came. Just then, in his mind the words of Pope John Paul, a modern pope and a true man of peace, returned to him, "the Earth was created subject to futility and in the daily struggle of good versus evil, the greatest fear, is the disappearance of hope." In his heart at that moment, he made a pledge to God and himself. If it's God's will for him to be delivered from this trial, he will honor Father Patrick's passing by living a life worthy of his faithful friend and mentor, he will no longer live his life in neutral feeling sorry for himself, he will strive to achieve God's best for however long this life's journey lasts so he can one day hear those meaningful words, "well done good and faithful servant, enter in."

Chapter Fifteen

Maggie's Prayers Are Heard

Meanwhile Frankie and Libby were working with the local authorities. The police were understandably preoccupied with the kidnapping of the Governor. Any consideration for information afforded to the missionaries coming down the pipeline was due to the fact that the priests and the Governor were presumed to be together. Top officials of the government were awaiting new intelligence anticipating to hear from the kidnappers with demands, political or otherwise. Strangely this seemed to be an isolated incident, an overthrow of the government was not expected because currently everything was quiet, militarily speaking. For the Governor to be snatched during daylight hours right in his own quarters meant there are those on the inside of the government who are sympathetic toward the kidnappers. It is difficult to maintain loyalty inside regimes where payola can be an effective tool in undermining the powers that be.

Upon hearing the news, Angela took a leave of absence, booked two flights to Africa and stood knocking on Sister Maggie's door at the convent. "I know it's late but may I please speak to Sister Maggie? Please, it's urgent!" Angela pleaded with frightened urgency in her voice. Angela waited inside mustering all the composure she could to be strong for

Sister Maggie. She tightly held back her tears the entire time she drove there. It frightened her to realize she doesn't even remember driving, she prayerfully thanked God for the angels she knows must have been stationed around her the entire way. As Sister Maggie walked quickly down the long corridor she could read the expression on Angela's face, analogous to the sixth sense of a mother's heart. "What's wrong?" Sister Maggie shouted. "Haven't you seen the news?" Angela questioned. "No, we're sheltered from the outside here, Angela." Sister Maggie shifted her weight after embracing Angela. "Of course, I'm sorry. I know that." Angela appeared confused. "Angela, sit down here, what in the world is wrong?" Sister Maggie pressed on, "is it that new young man you're dating, Dustin?" Angela broke into a sob and shouted, "No! No! It's Father Francis! He's been kidnapped!" Without saying a word, Sister Maggie grabbed her by the hand and whisked her around the corner to a candle lit prayer room with a cross at one end in front of a stained glass window. "Don't you want to hear?" Angela questioned. "No, I want to pray. I want you to pray with me," Sister Maggie insisted. "But I've got plane tickets for Africa, I've taken a leave of absence," Angela asserted. "We will go but first right now we need to kneel and pray," Sister Maggie said in an even tempered tone.

Angela was always so amazed by Sister Maggie's ability to not be overcome when unforeseen things happened and wondered if Maggie was putting on a strong facade for her sake during this trial. Maggie's resolve to immediately turn to God without hesitation impressed Angela as she helped her pack her things in order to leave, having concluded her heartfelt prayers, for the moment. Even though Angela's news didn't paint a rosy picture, Sister Maggie relied on her state of mind that turned Father Francis' safekeeping over to God on a daily basis. The details didn't really matter because either Francis was in God's hands or he wasn't. So the same peace that Maggie went to bed with every night as she prayed for Francis shouldn't change because of circumstances. She explained this to Angela with the hope of giving her comfort in the knowledge of God's sovereignty.

"I wish I was handling this as well as you, Sister," Angela confessed as they drove through the night to catch the early morning flight out of the country. Angela knew that Sister Magggie was required to keep a current visa and a passport for missionary trips which were often sponsored by donors to the convent. Angela's passport is current because of business trips to Canada and the Americas. "You need to know, Angela, I'm praying for God's will through this. He wouldn't have allowed it to happen unless He's intended on turning what's meant for evil into good, we still need to be prepared for the consequences of praying for God's will to be done. Now I'm going to tell you something I remember from one of Father Francis' sermons. This is something that's good to hang on to right now about maintaining your sense of peace. Are you ready? You need to reach out and touch Jesus. In a moment of doubt touch the scars in His wrists, He didn't invite just Thomas long ago, the offer is still for us today. Angela, reach out and touch the Savior and feel the sacrifice of His wounds taken for you so you'll know His risen authority and His overwhelming power in your life. That's what Father Francis taught me, to know that God is God. Father Francis went to Africa expecting his need to be met and I'm praying that the peace that surpasses all understanding will be his safeguard. As I pray, my motives must be led by the Spirit of God as to the outcome that glorifies His name. Somehow I just know that God is filling Francis' dry well with living water, even as we speak." Sister Maggie proclaimed.

"I believe it, too!" Angela chimed in.

"I've felt a particular burden in prayer lately. I know it's our prayers that make the difference. I have to believe that, especially when I'm so far away from Francis. I feel close to him when I pray because I understand he's praying for me, too. That's how I know he's okay, Angela. I can feel his prayers and I believe he feels mine as well. Does that sound crazy?" Sister Maggie asked with a warm smile.

"No, I've always felt your prayers, both you and Father Francis. It's your prayers that have gotten me through some of the toughest times over the years," Angela said as she glanced in Sister Maggie's direction.

"Now Father Francis needs our prayers but even more importantly our praise to God as we thank Him with hearts full of faith in His perfect plan," Sister Maggie said as she leaned back and closed her eyes in a meditative moment.

Angela felt better just being in Sister Maggie's presence. She didn't feel as frantic and confused as she did on the way to the convent. She's always thought of herself as pretty strong but this news totally unhinged her because so many missionaries come and go on trips without incident. It's not until you hear about the terrible stories of Christians around the world standing up for their faith and even losing their lives in martyrdom when it hits home, some pay a higher price than others. She liked to think that God gave them a bigger measure of faith depending on their need. Right now she prayed that God would give Father Francis what he needs to make it through this trial. Little did she know, her prayers were being answered. In the shadow of the valley of death, Francis found comfort in the promise to those in despair who reach up with a trembling hand and grasp the eternal promise that God will never leave or forsake the one who calls him or herself Christian.

Chapter Sixteen

Loves Determination

Via cell phone and the unbridled determination of a strong woman of God, Maggie placed one call after another in order to organize a campaign that would coordinate forces all the way from the local parish to the Vatican itself along with governmental agencies reaching to the Pentagon and right up to the White House front steps. She spent every moment speaking with contacts in the medical field and in the media, in order to reach anyone willing to listen. She started a prayer chain through a few strategic contacts that lit a fire on the Internet which circled the globe. A fire informing many through the impassioned plea of one sincere nun whose faith led the charge to shut down the force of evil that dared to rear its ugly head against the only thing on her mind, Francis, a man of God and the man she loves.

The plight of a priest held captive sparked the imagination of the world as it watched intently after the execution of his traveling companion. Worldwide newscasts were heard as you walked through any airport and street corner papers were splashed with their front page coverage telling the story of the African Governor and his unwitting guests who were literally and figuratively caught in the cross fire of extortionists, emphasizing the dramatic danger of traveling in this part of the world on a mission of mercy.

Francis could not even imagine the global whirlwind of intrigue swirling outside the four corners of this building. After many days, he decided he must eat in order to survive, he had no appetite and grew weaker by the hour. He and the Governor realized because of the sounds they heard outside that they were in some kind of compound where other prisoners also were. "I'm happy to see you eating, my friend," the Governor said with fatigue. "It's amazing how quickly you lose weight when you feel like your body is shutting down," Father Francis observed. "The body will do what the mind tells it to. If you eat, you will feel better and get stronger," the Governor said as he finished the morsel on his tin plate.

As they discussed their predicament, the two men quickly cultivated a unique bond in just a few days. Francis' suspicion about the Governor's beliefs were confirmed as they set aside their titles of priest and official long enough to recognize they were two peas in a most unusual pod. The Governor shared about the depression he suffered under for so many years and how it led him to a moment of honesty when he realized the political power he desperately sought after was futile and fleeting. In Africa respect for authority oftentimes had more to do with the point of a gun than the dreams of one's own heart. The Governor finally understood that he was too small to make a real difference by himself in such a harsh political environment. After asking God to come into his life through accepting Jesus Christ into his heart he began to act righteously in an unrighteous cutthroat arena. Important people often ask hard questions of a leader whose life recently took a one hundred and eighty degree turnaround in tactics and policy. He gained the courage necessary to do this when a family member paid the ultimate price for sharing the truth with him. The Governor wouldn't comment any further about persecution and Francis understood it's hallowed ground in regard to their conversations. When he spoke of his story of conversion, the Governor's eyes glazed over and his voice grew faint. Francis realized the conversion of this politically important man was at a very high cost and that God is sure to use him mightily to change the face of his fellow Africans.

"I hear your questioning in your silence, my friend," the Governor said with a serious tone, "you are wondering where I get the nerve."

"For not knowing God for very long, you have taken great risks that you knew were very dangerous. How did you find the resolve?" Francis questioned honestly.

"The resolve to do what I know is right?" the Governor sat up and continued, "I knew I needed real answers to my questions. Answers not cloaked in mysterious terms of someday or somehow that depended on weak faith. This relative who shared strong faith with me told me to receive something that all Christians should have but don't always want because they're intimidated by authority and power not knowing what to do with it. But I am a man who was raised in the military. Learning from authority taught me to seek power my entire life. After praying for my salvation which is my authority, this person laid their hand on my head and prayed again. He did not pray for me to receive the baptism of water for repentance but the baptism of the Holy Spirit and fire, unquenchable fire that John the Baptist himself said would be imparted by the One who was to come after him, Jesus. As I have come to understand it since then this fire is the Baptism of the Holy Spirit, the Spirit who raised Christ from the dead. This power overcomes sin and adversity." As the Governor finished, the guards came in and took him away for his daily interrogation of extracting information and intimidation purposes.

Francis pondered the Governor's testimony and reflected on other conversations he's had over the years with colleagues about their particular tradition of water baptism. The Governor shared that when he was water baptized he understood this to represent his dying to his sin and the risen victory. His eyes brightened when he spoke of his resurrection from the grave with Christ. Francis won't deny the fact that this man has risked his entire way of life because this experience revolutionized his spirit. When speaking with the Governor his spirit was aroused as he recalled Acts 19 which was puzzling to him but now made more sense. The chapter speaks of Paul addressing disciples in Ephesus and asking them if they'd received the Holy Spirit when they first believed? They responded that they'd never heard of the Holy Spirit and had been baptized in John the Baptist's baptism of repentance. Paul shared with them that John's baptism of repentance was true telling them to believe in Him who came after, that is, Jesus Christ and when Paul baptized them in the Name of Christ Jesus and laid hands on them the Holy Spirit came upon them and they prophesied and spoke in diverse tongues.

These words flooded Francis' mind because he had studied them many times over and had debated pastor friends about this. Only now, however, do these words begin to penetrate his spirit. After a few hours of sleep, Francis was woken up by the screams of someone being tortured. He couldn't recognize who it was and was disturbed that it coincided with the Governor's absence. Feeling more alone now as this was happening caused a panic to ensue in his soul. He wondered how he would handle being tortured and found himself in an in-between place of wanting to live for his faith and questioning his willingness to die for it. Stress took its toll as Francis said a silent prayer and sobbed uncontrollably. Suddenly the entire room filled with brilliant light and he wondered if a floodlight was being shone through the narrow windows. But then he realized there's no apparent heat emanating from it only an amazing peace, the peace that surpasses all understanding. He began to cry out and involuntarily spoke in an unknown language. Burden after burden, layer upon layer of worry, fear and sorrow left him like a poisonous snake skin shedding from him that had been clinging to him for years. He felt the impact of God's spirit flowing all over and through him in waves as his soul regurgitated many hateful things that were said to him in his life, beginning in childhood. Little things, big things, seemingly unimportant events and soul wrenching crisis points that had never healed completely. He lifted his head up and pictured the shriveled man he envisioned a few nights ago. Francis then stood up and declared, "I am not that man, I am a new creation in Christ." As the words fell from his lips, he felt the weak enemy leave him and the strength of the Lord gird him up. A strength that didn't just come from a meal or an isolated word of encouragement but a lifelong strength that never fails and always prevails, which fuels the embers of a fire that can't be distinguished by mere circumstances. This is a forever assurance like a lighthouse in a storm whose lamp always stays lit night and day, come what may. This encounter left Francis knowing in his spirit that God will not only deliver him from this current trial but left him with the revelation that his path to achieve great and mighty things for God is sure and steadfast.

Chapter Seventeen

An Amazing Deliverance

Over the next couple of weeks, Francis' fear of torture coming to its fruition, still played on his nerves, however, for some reason he was spared this unspeakable torment. The kidnappers were more interested in the Governor in regards to extracting specific information about comrades held by the government and their interest in having them released through an exchange. The mere fact that they're willing to torture a subject they have a desire to barter with gives insight to the reality that they're a fringe element, not very well versed in the political upheaval that's created by torturing someone who's a valuable asset in such negotiations. This means they're radical and unpredictable and have little fear of repercussions including their own demise.

Francis did what he could to nurse the Governor's wounds including sharing his own daily allottment of water with him. He didn't use any of the Governor's water during nursing because the Governor needed as much strength as possible for any chance of survival. The torture techniques were hideous and mercenary in nature; either these terrorists didn't have access to medical help or they didn't realize how close to death their precious prisoner was. The Governor spent a lot of time unconscious and Francis was frustrated that he couldn't communicate better with their captors to request the most basic supplies required to help his prisonmate. Francis stayed awake into the early morning hours as he monitored the Governor's pulse and breathing to determine his heart rate and whether penumonia might be setting in from swallowing so much blood, the byproduct of inadvertently breathing liquid into the lungs from a specific torture technique.

Francis was startled when the door swung open one day and two women cloaked head to foot in fundamentalist garb were allowed in by the guards. Only their eyes could be seen peering out as they carried what appeared to be First Aid supplies. The doors were closed but a guard stood outside watching through the door's peephole to monitor the situation closely. Evidently their captors were having second thoughts about the health of the Governor since his condition was not improving. The two women quickly moved to the Governor's side and began attending to him. Francis didn't realize right away that this particular visit by these two women was no coincidence. It was a worldwide answer to prayer from hundreds if not thousands of those who've joined in the daily petitioning of God for the safe return of Father Francis.

Over the last couple of weeks as the two men were isolated with only each other's company, a sequence of events quickly brought about divine appointments as Sister Maggie arrived in Africa and began meeting with top level officials who'd been garnered through her contacts due to countless phone calls. An influential business billionaire with ties to Africa set into motion dealings of a covert plan to coordinate with governmental officials to infiltrate the terrorist camp. Everyone involved had a stake in this international incident being resolved peacefully. Locating the compound happened rather quickly once enough palms were greased, setting the wheels in motion for specific infomation to reach the captives. The problem was finding and trusting someone with the information because there was always the possibility of the double cross, payola can work both ways with some locals who are all too eager to work both sides.

Public outrage and American political forces put pressure on the governments of the U.S. and Africa to do away with any roadblocks, real or perceived that could prevent a less than positive outcome. The attention of the world was keenly focused on Father Francis' plight. The initial news stories understandably were about the Governor's kidnapping but then turned into a political hot potato when the Vatican started moving in and waving the banner of justice for Father Francis; the poster child for persecution of Christians around the world. The amazing ball of public opinion began when Sister Maggie initiated the Internet campaign and by her initial phone calls, she grabbed the media's attention and possessed direct influence. The proverbial ball was in her court and she was the powerbroker who called the shots.

One of the women spoke to Francis motioning him to come closer then directed her attention to the guard speaking to him. Francis didn't realize that she told the guard he's coming over to hold the Governor down when they set his broken arm, it's important that he lay still. The guard responded then turned around with his back to the door unconcerned with the priest helping in the procedure. Francis knelt down beside the Governor on his bedroll, the woman took his hand and put it on the shoulder of the Governor as if to say "hold him down". Her companion held the Governor down on the adjacent side. The woman pulled down the veil covering her face in order to take a deep breath and glanced up at Francis for a second then pulled the Governor's arm violently as it snapped back into place. The Governor groaned and passed out again. Without missing a beat, the other woman who held the Governor down slipped a note into Francis' hand and squeezed it. He felt a gigantic tingle go through his arm as he automatically turned his palm up and opened his hand to reveal a small unfolded note. He could read it even in the dim light. It said, "I'm here." Just then, she pulled down her veil and Maggie's sweet smile made Francis' eyes feel like they were popping out of his head. She immediately grabbed his arm hard enough to cause pain stifling his reaction as he momentarily forgot the danger all of them were in. She placed another note in his hand and mouthed the words, "I love you." Maggie glanced over to the other woman to signal it's imperative for them to leave right away. They accomplished their mission by tending to the Governor and also passed the important message on to Francis.

Before he even had a chance to think they were gone, it was all just like a dream. He sat by the Governor stunned by what had just happened. What in the world was Maggie doing in his cell so far from home? He had no comprehension of what God orchestrated and accomplished through Maggie for him. It was so great to see Maggie's smiling face, even if just for a second. Now that he's thought about it, there was something familiar about the way she moved and squeeezed his hand but her being there was so far out of context, he didn't think for a moment that one of these two women could be his dear, sweet Maggie delivering a message to him for his escape to freedom. He waited until they were out of sight and made sure no one was peering through the hole to read the crumpled note. The message simply said that in three days he must get his captors to move him to an underground bunker that according to military intelligence is understood to be solitary confinement and a torture chamber. The note also indicated that the Governor was going to be moved by his captors and consequently rescued at a different location. The important but dangerous thing Francis was being asked to do was to incite these terrorists to action before the Governor's removal two days from now, otherwise there wouldn't be any reason to move him since he'd already be isolated due to the Governor's absense. In order for this plan to work, Francis needed to give his captors a reason to torture him. Once the Governor was moved and Francis safe underground, the military would infiltrate with heavy artillery to devastate the compound and retrieve the priest. Its a bold plan that made Francis very nervous. He spent most of the day prayerfully contemplating his sitation. He reflected back over the last couple of weeks where he encountered the presence of God so intensely, he felt as though he glowed like an expectant mother due to God's glorious presence. His spirit was rather light and unencumbered, his only concern was the Governor and his health. He'd been interceding in prayer and tending the best he could to the Governor's wounds. Francis decided to wait until the dawn of the second day and began singing "Jesus, Jesus, Jesus, There's Just Something About That Name." He continued throughout the morning singing praises to God until he heard rustling outside and voices speaking quickly and sounding annoyed. The voices died down and Francis continued singing at the top of his lungs. He felt a wonderful sensation come over him as he sang. He pictured Paul in prison singing God's glory. Tears began to flow as immense happiness filled his spirit and unspeakable joy invaded his soul with profound praise. Francis was lost in the moment and never realized how much time had passed when the doors violently flew open and two guards came in. One guard swung his rifle in the air and butted the gun down just missing Francis' temple. As it struck him, the last words heard trailing from his lips were "forgive them, Father..."

While he was unconscious they dragged him to the underground bunker then moved the Governor by jeep to an undisclosed location. By the end of the second day, Francis woke up with a massive headache and a welt on the side of his head that couldn't be touched it was so painful. He found himself in a dungeon with absolutely no light and tried hard to focus enough to figure out his surroundings but the strain only made his head spin. His stomach tightened as he heard men screaming outside and banging which led him to believe his time was coming nearer to being tortured. Francis prayed under his breath and thought of St. Stephen and the great privilege to be martyred for one's faith. He chuckled at his persecutors who didn't have anything in common with him except for their understanding of the concept of martyrdom for one's beliefs. How ironic. If they could only know the perfect unconditional love of God that didn't come into the world to condemn it but to save it from sin, then they too, would be set free from the bondage of religious legalism that leads to opression and destruction in the hands of unrighteous men. Feeling like a young Isaac laid prostrate across the sacrificial fire of his father, Abraham, Francis heard the deafening sound of artillery like a ram in the thicket coming to deliver him. Francis fell to his knees and placed his face against the ground. He thanked God first for his loving act of grace when He sent Jesus to save him from iniquity. Because of his encounter with the Holy Spirit, even in this ironic moment of relief from torture, he was most grateful for his eternal life as opposed to his carnal existence that is fleeting and temporary. This point was repeatedly driven home hard during his trial here. As the American soldiers carried him out of the bunker, Francis' face illuminated God's goodness and he could be heard muttering the words, "Nothing can separate me from the love of God, nothing."

Francis opened his eyes and for a moment he believed he'd died and gone to Heaven because the first face he saw was Father Patrick's. "What happened? Father P, weren't you shot and killed? You're supposed to be dead!" Francis tried to sit up putting his hand to his battered brow. He saw Maggie, Angela, Frankie and Libby with Father Patrick all around his bedside. Maggie leaned over and spoke into his ear, "Psychological terrorism, Francis, emotional torture."

"Well, it worked!" Francis said half smiling while tears ran down his cheeks. "I'm so relieved we're both okay. Is the Governor safe?"

"Yes, he needs surgery but he's expected to fully recover," Angela explained.

Maggie said, "Angela helped me to coordinate everything, Francis. I couldn't have done it without her." Francis squeezed Angela's hand as Maggie leaned over and whispered into his ear again, "You went to an awful lot of trouble getting yourself kidnapped and all, just to get me to come and be with you in Africa." Francis let out a boisterous belly laugh and Maggie started to answer his questions about how God's amazing grace made a way for them to all be together again. Angela explained to Francis that he's become somewhat of a celebrity and that accepting an audience with the Pope is just one of many things he'd need to consider as he recovered from the ordeal. Father Patrick interrupted by informing Francis that Larry King wants to interview him.

"Larry King? Really?" Francis grinned as the wheels turned in his mind.

"What are you thinking, Francis?" Maggied asked.

"I dreamt about the fawn again and I think all of this is God turning evil into good so we can tell people about fighting AIDS with liquid nutrition," Francis surmised.

They all started talking at once with excitement. Angela said, "We've already got the Internet infrastructure. I bet there's a million Christians praying for you, maybe even more." Father P indicated, "And as you tell your story, I'm sure there will be donations pouring in for FAWN once they realize the desperate need." Maggie joined in the excitement, "God knows what He's doing, Francis. There's no one better at championing this cause than you. We better get that bump on your forehead healed before you appear in front of all those cameras."

"Please, my head is already spinning just talking about this. But it is exciting! Who would have ever had thought that God might open doors for a platform for FAWN using the story of a kidnapped priest?" Francis wondered.

Frankie said intently, "Who knows? Maybe you'll get a book deal, Father," and Libby said fancifully, "The next thing you know they'll be making a movie of your life."

As he laid there shaking his head affirmatively at each of them, Francis took his friends hands as they created a circle of prayer around his hospital bed. When they concluded praising God for His faithfulness, Francis told them that the foundation is to be built upon love and he doesn't know any other circle of people who'd make a better board of directors for FAWN, not only because of their fondness for him but their unbridled passion for spreading God's love across the ocean in a land called Africa.

Chapter Eighteen

I'm Not Ashamed of My Love For You

The next few days was a whirlwind with Francis and Father Patrick being transferred to an American military base in Germany where a complete medical examination was in order including general and also very specific blood testing for anything from Malaria to HIV/AIDS tests to the most unlikely and rare diseases known to mankind. Even though all parties involved had their shots, including Maggie and Angela, no stone was left unturned with respect to giving the priests a clean bill of health. Francis wouldn't even consider accepting the Pope or Larry King's invitation without the thorough debriefing from the American officials who demanded a detailed account of the men's harrowing experiences. Angela decided not to accompany Maggie to Germany. She gave Maggie the letter she had written and left on Francis' desk. Maggie couldn't think about leaving Francis during this complicated time when so many important decisions about the future needed to be made. A nun certainly doesn't have the resources for such a leave of absence on the international scene, however, Sister Maggie never spent any money while working as a nurse outside the convent life this many years and had accumulated a substantial nest egg. Maggie was allowed to go with Francis to Germany on the military transport but was responsible for her own accommodations at a hotel near the military base during the debriefing. Father Patrick, however, suffered substantial hearing loss by being held near deafening enemy artillery exercises during his captivity. He was moved to a facility in Sweden that specializes in Tinnitus with regard to causality and treatment for the hearing impaired. Francis noticed they all had spoken very loudly for Father Patrick to understand what was being said and he was relieved that his old friend and mentor will be treated by the best money can buy. They wished each other well as they strongly embraced like two warriors who've been through hell together.

Over the next couple of weeks, Angela stayed in contact with Maggie and informed her of her correspondence with the Larry King Live Show and the Vatican in regards to keeping them informed of when the two priests would be available. She let them know that Father Patrick isn't interested until he's found out the extent of his hearing loss and whether it's temporary or not. Francis was shielded from the blitz of the media's vain attempts to speak with him thanks to the military's strident rules and regulations. Once he was assigned to his quarters he asked if Maggie could be given clearance to visit him there. His request was granted in a few days after filtering through the proper channels and a time was appointed for her arrival.

"I'm impressed with your suite, Father Francis," Sister Maggie said with wide eyes as she entered through the double doors, "Is it okay meeting here?"

"I think fraternization is discouraged only when it comes to military personnel. I suspect our status as priest and nun puts us above suspicion," Francis speculated.

"I don't know, can we be trusted?" Maggie laughed as she embraced him with a kiss on his now blushing cheek.

"Usually, but I have to admit you're a sight for sore eyes, Mag-pie. I read the letter you gave me yesterday. I've spent so many hours thinking about us," he reflected.

"Me, too, especially when Angela shared with me her fantasies about what it would have been like if we'd been a conventional family," she responded.

"Did you ever wonder?" he asked sheepishly motioning for her to sit in one of the two chairs in front of the parlor room fireplace.

"I'm not sure we should talk about this in such an intimate setting. What kind of military base is this anyway?" she asked.

"Well, first of all, these are my quarters. It's important to get the military vernacular right, you know," he said laughing, "evidently they often have important officials here who need appropriate accommodations and protection with high level security."

"It's nice to know someone is benefiting from our tax dollars hard at work," she asserted.

"I noticed you didn't answer my questions, very evasive of you," he softly said.

"Well, I'll tell you what I told Angela, there's not much point in crying over spilt milk," she said with equal tenderness.

"First of all, you are lactose intolerant and so it's not likely you'd cry over milk, spilt or any other kind. Second of all, your choice of metaphor leads me to believe you did cry about it, not to mention your letter. Besides it seems to me I remember you were the one who broke the wedding engagement," Francis said trying to corner her.

"Well, someone had to. We both knew that God's call to you was too strong to be ignored," she insisted.

"Do you ever wonder how many people God calls who are in the same boat but instead decide to selfishly choose love?" Francis continued his attempt to stir the melancholy fire.

"Well, my dear Francis, I don't have to tell someone like you who knows so much about the topic, there's nothing really selfish about love, is there?" Maggie inquired with slight whimsy.

"I don't know, there's been an awful lot of damage done to people in love, not being able to think straight and making decisions with their heads in the clouds," Francis suggested.

"I like to think our relationship, all be it unconsummated, goes much deeper than an infatuation and that so called real love hastily brings about personal and professional ruin for many," Maggie rebutted.

"Well, I have a confession to make. When I wasn't sure if I'd come out of this alive, I couldn't stand the thought that I'd never really have a chance to show you how much I love you," Francis said intently.

"Why Father Francis, feel free to show me now," Maggie giggled as she winked at him.

"You know what I mean, not like that," Francis said sternly.

"No, too bad?" Maggie said, having way too much fun.

"I'm not going to let you rattle me," he said vehemently.

"Do you feel rattled?" Maggie asked batting her eyelashes at him.

"Of course I've always wanted you in every single way, but please let me finish. I mean in the way a lifetime says I love you, where we wake up and fall asleep together year in and year out, knowing you're not just two ships passing in the night," he said gently.

"I know, I'd rather us be one big boat, too. It's been a heavy price to pay. Are you saying it's been too big a price?" she inquired.

"I'm not questioning God's will for us and that doesn't mean · I have to like it," he said respectfully.

"Well, just for the record, I don't like it either," Maggie said and she zipped out of her chair, sat in his lap and said, "I love you and I'm not ashamed of it."

At this very moment, time and space intersected and a kiss that waited for so many years to be realized like butterflies fluttering when released, brought the lips of these two servants together in an overwhelming embrace. It was a combination of Agape or platonic love for one another and humankind but also passionate love between the two of them just as it was meant to be when two souls give themselves so freely to each other. They didn't know it could be like this, they didn't remember their kisses being so sweet when they were courting. Maybe it's because their love had been cultivated over the years through so many trials and without the complication of hurt feelings that sometimes goes hand in hand with intimate romantic relationships. It has been the best and the worst of times, they were always free of the pettiness a daily love life would often churn up when not properly cultivated yet they were deprived of the richness of the blessings of oneness in sharing it all, not just in part, in God's blessed union. The sweetness cannot be appreciated without the bitter in the bittersweet nature of living a lifetime of love together as a married couple.

Maybe they would have gone on for years before Francis went to Africa and Maggie to the convent. But the separation and recent dramatic events proved what they did not consider before, that they could no longer live apart. Francis shared with Maggie the idea of bringing up the hot button topic of priests marrying at his meeting with the Pope, he also knew it was a long shot but believed because of so many years of controversy surrounding the Church, the time might be right to add his proverbial two cents to the conversation. She suggested a strategic plan of action to put pressure on the Vatican using their own story to rally supporters through a series of interviews. Francis, however, worried the Vatican would view this as social or political pressure that it rarely responded well to. Putting the cart before the horse could sabotage everything and Francis could lose his audience altogether. They reminded themselves that the ultimate goal was to bring attention to the plight of AIDS victims and not let their personal feelings in any way be a stumbling block to God's mercy and love being shown to Africa through their work with FAWN. At the same time, their relationship had changed and they couldn't ignore that. They decided to be prayerful about their next step and to see what opportunities may arise that could be a providential sign.

Chapter Nineteen

The Decision to Go Public

Back in the United States, Angela was interrupted frequently by the media for details of the amazing story and they were increasingly impatient waiting for answers to their questions, Angela could only continually repeat that because of military protocol information was prevented from being released until all aspects of the investigation were final. The international frenzy this front page story had created was only part of Angela's headache. Good old Widow Bridges was beside herself regarding the news about Sister Maggie joining Father Francis in Africa. This information was widespread in the media and the speculation about them that was once within the four walls of the parish was now being bantered about nationally and internationally. Widow Bridges was demanding Father Francis be immediately reassigned because of her worry about the parish being painted with the broad brush of indecency. The fact is Widow Bridges had nobody but herself to thank because in her usual way of overreacting, she gave a phone interview to a national tabloid that began an Internet buzz about a too friendly priest and nun. So Francis and Maggie's conversation about managing how information would impact their plans seemed futile now with Widow Bridges having untied the knot herself and brought even more unfavorable attention to the parish. The controversy about priests and nuns marrying had already reached a fevered pitch to the point that the mainstream media had little choice but to address the red hot topic head on whether they considered the tired old argument worth addressing or not. But no matter the topic, unresolved issues have a tendency to resurface for debate time and time again.

Angela placed a call to Francis explaining that he might as well do the Larry King Live interview on TV now because the speculation is probably going to get more intense anyway. At the very least he could promote his passion to help Africa. Francis agreed after talking with Maggie and told Angela they'll both appear together to address the kidnapping and their relationship but wanted to make sure a segment on the hour long show is exclusively dedicated to talking about AIDS management through nutrition. Angela was concerned about their fielding questions about their relationship but Francis assured her that they've prayerfully decided that full disclosure is the best policy to avoid the story gaining legs on its own.

Angela called back the following day to let them know the Larry King Show TV producers wanted to do a satellite interview as soon as possible because they don't want to wait until the two returned to America. Evidently they got wind of a magazine TV show that was willing to pay one million dollars for their story in a pre-taped interview there in Germany. Francis was able to reach Maggie on an extension to discuss this prospect with Angela who had already received the offer on their behalf.

"A million dollars. A million dollars?" Maggie said with a strained voice. "I can't even figure out how many cans of liquid nutrition that would buy," Francis said briskly.

Skipping to the importance of her call, Angela started out by saying, "You want to make sure you don't undercut your credibility. In terms of this kind of international attention, you've got to realize everybody wants a piece of this story, that very fact means they'll be trying to work every angle to separate themselves from the pack. Ethics aren't exactly at the top of the list when it comes to meeting a hard deadline for their editors or producers."

"What exactly does that mean, Angela?" Maggie asked.

Francis answered for her, "They'll make us look like opportunists even if our hearts are in the right place. Angela's right, we've got to look at the long haul and make sure the FAWN foundation remains a credible influence for hope in the future."

Angela responded by saying, "It's true, bad press will close a lot of doors that could lead to even more than a million dollars of financial support. The media attention alone is worth more than that. But I'm also worried about you guys. Are you ready for the questions about your relationship? You wouldn't believe what everyone's saying out there."

Maggie said in a calm voice, "We're going to tell the truth. That's all we can do and hope people will understand."

"Keep in mind, the talking heads will be on every medium from all sides of this nun-priest thing. If you don't answer the questions just the right way, it could blow up in your faces," said Angela to clarify further.

Francis said intently, "I know it's a calculated risk but we've got to believe that this platform is something God's brought about and Maggie's right, we'll just tell our story."

Maggie asserted, "At least it's a live show and there won't be any funny editing going on."

"That's true," Angela said, "but don't forget that clips of the show will end up on You Tube for everyone to see over and over, forever. Crossing this line will mean there's no return. I don't have to tell you that your careers in the Catholic Church will more than likey be over."

Francis concurred by saying, "Maybe so but we need to focus on the bigger picture. This is an awful big spotlight."

"I've been working on setting up a website for FAWN, www.fightingaids.org. It should be ready soon. Do you want me to create a link to a web page that provides a written summary of the story of your relationship?" Angela asked.

"Normally I'd say that's not appropriate but under these unusual circumstances I think it would go a long way in providing the truth from our perspectives," Francis said and Maggie agreed, "As long as the wording is delicate."

"Both of you should begin writing it out so it's in your own words, please, this will also help to prepare you a little for what you might say during the interview. We could also use video clips from interviews on the website as a way to control the story somewhat," Angela inferred.

Francis said, "That's wishful thinking I'm afraid, but the idea of writing our own story is a good one and we'll get to work on it."

Angela continued on, "I will also be setting up a tasteful donation aspect of the website as well. I have a Christian attorney friend whose firm can handle the specifics, if you like."

"I don't know what we'd do without you, Angela." Francis graciously said, and Maggie added, "It's so true, it's nice to know we won't be going through this alone."

As they concluded their call, Francis thought about all the attention from the media; not only fanning the flame with respect to priests and nuns being unable to marry but this will certainly rekindle the prolonged public strife regarding sexual misconduct in the Catholic Church that is unwelcome attention from the Vatican's perspective.

Francis always kept his personal opinion to himself and his response to celibacy was part of the commitment to his ministry, he stayed pure in this area because of Maggie's and his like mindedness over the years. He knows others fall prey to earthly desires that are either carnal in nature or come about through nuns and priests working in close proximity and becoming too familiar but he and Maggie fell in love before they took their vocational vows of commitment to God. The dramatic events they just lived through brought them closer to God and to each other, strengthening their love with a new bond through a change of heart. He may have been only rationalizing but wanted to believe that God turned evil into good by saving him from the kidnappers and the attention on their relationship was a part of His perfect will for them. Francis realized that the attention for FAWN was going to come anyway because of the kidnapping but he was unsettled with the portrayal of their relationship, he felt it could overshadow the spotlight on God and His glory. As he prayed, Francis relied on his new experience with the Holy Spirit to speak from his heart. He felt a peace bubbling up through his spirit. He admitted to the Lord he didn't really understand what was happening with everything but promised to rest in God's perfect solitude as he took one step at a time with a firm desire to be led by the Spirit of God.

Chapter Twenty

The Proposal Heard Round the World

Once the military completely debriefed Francis, he and Maggie spent time site seeing together in Germany. They received word that Father Patrick was responding well to treatment and the prognosis for his hearing is a positive recovery. Angela contacted Francis a few days later and said she lined up the Satellite TV interview with Larry King for tomorrow night. The anxiety was palpable as Francis and Maggie prepared. They visited a number of Catholic churches as they continued to pray that their words be of God during the interview. When the time came, while makeup was being applied to each of them in separate rooms and the hot lights were turned on an hour before the live feed, their stomachs were doing flip flops. Not so much about telling their story but telling it to so many people at one time. The promotional spots that had been running over the last few days in anticipation of this broadcast were certainly sensational. The buzz reached an international fevered pitch on TV, talk radio and on the Internet. Conversation went from generic to very specific opinions about Francis and Maggie's relationship. It's often difficult to set the record straight when the cement of commentary has begun to harden and the facts are often viewed as merely inconsequential by comparison.

Unknown to Francis and Maggie, Larry King introduced a high-ranking Bishop from the Vatican whose image was being fed live from Rome, Italy. In the studio was a retired American military general giving perspective on the kidnapping and rescue. After 45 minutes of back and forth between all parties involved, the only aspects discussed so far were the details about what happened with respect to what led up to the kidnapping, the confinement, the escape and rescue.

Larry King then announced that he'd be extending the live program for another half hour because of the complexity of the story. The producers also knew that going off the air without addressing the personal relationship between this nun and priest would be unacceptable. Larry King is an expert at moving the show along by asking one pointed question after another but each detail of the story was so important to the human interest portion that skipping anything wasn't practical. Francis successfully gave a testimony about this spiritual experience and felt good about God being glorified through it all. During the break the producer approached Francis to let him know they'd be interested in having him back to talk even more specifically about the implication of a priest who seemed to couch his experience in Pentecostal terms. Francis leaned over to Maggie and whispered that he hoped the second part of the program would go as well as the first. She responded by implying that they could probably expect a call from Jerry Springer after this next segment. He nervously grinned at her as the cue came up from the commercial break.

"We're back speaking with Father Francis and Sister Maggie. There are reports that you are more than just a nun and a priest when it comes to your personal relationship. Is it true that she turned your marriage proposal down early in your relationship and that's the reason you became a priest?" Larry King asked concisely.

Maggie responded on behalf of Francis without hesitation, "Certainly not..."

"Here, let me," Francis said as he placed his hand on her arm, "We were nurses together and had fallen in love but Maggie recognized that I felt a strong call to do God's work."

"I wasn't going to get in the way of that call. God had to be first," Maggie said briskly.

Larry King then asked, "According to our local sources at your parish, you have been intimately involved for a long time. Is that true? And if so, what's changed?"

Maggie returned fired, "We've never been intimate!"

Francis interrupted, "No, but something has changed. During my captivity I realized how my cup was only half full without Maggie being more a part of my life. It's not good that man be alone, that's why God created Eve, to be a helpmate," Maggie squeezed Francis' hand still resting on her arm.

Larry King continued, "Does this mean you're challenging the Catholic Church's authority in the matter of nuns and priests not being able to marry?"

Before Francis could answer the question, they went to station break and let the audience know that he'll give the answer to that question when they return. Maggie leaned over and whispered her concern in Francis' ear about the way the interview was going. He assured her that everything would be alright.

"We're back with Father Francis and Sister Maggie. Let me ask the Bishop a question before we get Father Francis' answer. The more we hear about this couple, Bishop, the feedback from a vast majority of Protestants and Catholics around the world who have been closely watching this story can't help but feel as though Father Francis and Sister Maggie are somehow meant to be together. Do you think there will ever be a time when the Catholic Church might consider changing its stance on this issue?"

"I cannot speak directly for the Pope. However I can speak from the perspective of the Vatican's support of traditional roles for priests and nuns with respect to celibacy."

Larry King cross examined, "With so much scandal regarding this issue and the overwhelming reports of abuse in almost every aspect of sexuality in the ranks of the Catholic Chruch, isn't it arrogant of the church to not be willing to reexamine its policy? Why don't they have a Third Vatican Council or something? I think this is big enough."

Francis interrupted, "I don't know if that will happen, Larry. I'm sorry but church dogma in this matter has become more important than the biblical example, both old and New Testament. We keep arguing the same points back and forth but never reach a conclusion that's legitimately resolved by the true nature of God."

Larry King responded with a question, "What do you mean by the true nature of God?"

Francis placed one arm around Maggie and said, "It's love, Larry. It's simply love. It's not the twisted love that mankind musters up. I know it's not popular but the devil's in the business of distorting what God made holy and he's doing a find job of brainwashing us by confusing love with sexual self satisfaction that doesn't resemble the healthy pattern God laid out for humanity."

Larry King asked, "But aren't you distorting love as a priest and nun?"

Maggie responded, "No, because God set the standard to be one man and one woman serving Him together."

Francis continued, "Again, I know it's not politically correct but if we as a people want to prevent one generation after another from decaying into a cesspool of sin that undermines the health of everyone at large, we've got to recognize that using the word love for every type of unnatural affection dilutes the nature of the purity God intended love to represent."

Larry King asked the Bishop, "Bishop, do you agree with Father Francis' statement?"

The Bishop responded by saying, "That's the very thing the Catholic Church is trying to do by keeping its priests and nuns pure and holy."

Maggie said, "But how can I, as a nun, effectively minister to someone when my own limitations of understanding the complexity of relationships in marriage and having children is inadequate? I can give them spiritual advice based on biblical precepts but everyone knows that creating an illusion of purity, as noble as it sounds, doesn't put the suffering at ease, when I cannot relate to their issues."

The Bishop rebutted, "There must be role models in order for people to recognize they're sinners."

Francis responded, "But that's the point, celibate priests and nuns can't be a practical role model for the Godly pattern of marriage. During my captivity I came to the understanding that we as the Church have been trying to do what God's spirit has intended to do by leading us into righteous living through the same kind of power that brought Christ out of the garden tomb. When Jesus ascended to Heaven, He said, 'I will send the comforter who is the Holy Spirit.'"

Maggie continued, "And even Father Francis doesn't know that I have had a similar spiritual renewal and now understand what Jesus meant when He told His disciples He had to return to His Heavenly Father so His spirit could dwell in the believer's heart."

Francis went further and continued by saying, "The church was never meant to be a heavy handed watch dog for God. . Mercy and love are reflected through a heart that's been humbled and became transparent to do the work of Heaven. Pretending we're perfect as clergy is hypocritical. Instead of a role model we end up being an embarrassment because we have no purity outside of a personal relationship with Jesus and conforming into His likeness through obedience to the Holy Spirit's guidance."

The final few minutes of the program brought the night to a close. Francis and Maggie were individually praising God for putting the words into their mouths especially since they didn't really have a clue what they were going to say. Their quick responses took Larry King by surprise and before he could think of another question, Father Francis and Sister Maggie's points were already made.

Larry King asked, "Finally, what about the future for you both?"

Francis looked at Maggie sweetly and proceeded to get down on one knee and asked, "Will you marry me?"

Maggie didn't even blink and threw her arms around Francis' neck and said, "The last time you asked me, I said no, but now I'm saying yes in front of the whole world."

Larry King concluded with an engagement announcement for Francis and Maggie, he apologized for not having more time for the couple to elaborate on what they believe the ramifications of their union as nun and priest might mean and how the church will respond. He did, however, make an open invitation on air to have them in the studio when they get back to the United States.

If anyone thought the firestorm of controversy swirled before the interview, it was nothing like what was conspiring as the lights dimmed at each satellite location. The next few days brought a number of organizations on every side of the issue with public demonstrations that included high profile religious, political and even the entertainment industry propagating their own opinions and agendas. Francis was disappointed that everything happened so fast in the interview and the fact that FAWN was competely overlooked. The producers just brushed him off when, during the station breaks, he continued to remind them that there was supposed to be a segment dedicated to the AIDS issue. When the 90 minute program finished, they appeased Francis by telling him that they would have them back for an entire hour just on that topic alone. He told them he wanted to bring his missionary friends from Africa, if possible, and Father Patrick as well.

Maggie reminded Francis because of the publicity now he could feel free to pick any venue he liked to get the message out about FAWN but Francis also understood there's no bigger audience than the show they were just on.

On a lighter note, Francis and Maggie felt such a sense of freedom in having proclaimed their love for one another and even though they're both very private people, they couldn't help feeling relieved of a burden so many years in the making. They felt as though a wrong had been righted through finally admitting they can't live without one another. They had subsequent conversations on their flight home bringing into question their love in relation to Catholic beliefs and the guilt that is so commonly associated with the do's and don'ts of traditional standards set by the church.

They were briefly shielded from the media through traveling by military transport but that was over now because they were taking a civilian flight for the last leg of their journey home. As they boarded the plane an outburst of applause took them by surprise. The senior flight attendant motioned them to return forward because the pilot had upgraded them from coach to first class. When they turned around a lady wagged her finger at them and told them what a disgrace they are to the faith, Francis and Maggie purposely were not wearing their normal attire trying to avoid as much attention as possible. They also knew they would more than likely hear from the parish board and the regional Catholic authority and until then Francis and Maggie will not know their status within the Catholic Church.

Except for their tie to Angela, in many ways they felt as though they set sail on a sea with no flag to fly by other than their determination to make a difference for Africa. Their new life's journey together holds the hope of their new found revelation, a vibrant faith conversion that each had undergone to navigate the choppy seas that continue to toss their vessel of divine destiny to and fro. They were physically exhausted by everything that happened over the last number of months and at the same time they were revitalized by the Morning Star leading them forward and beyond the horizon, a horizon waiting to be realized by a man and a woman holding one another's hands looking heavenward to follow the Morning Star named, Jesus.

Chapter Twenty One

AIDS Gets Personal

As the young blonde stewardess informed the passengers they'd be landing in about forty five minutes, Francis noticed an envelope edge attached to the envelope which held his medical records. It was sealed. He never opened it when he received the other medical records and thought it strange that he missed it before. It was smaller in size and caught in a loose fold of the other envelope. He detached it, his heart began to race when he saw the word CONFIDENTIAL in bold red ink typed across the center of the page,

Dear Reverend Francis Galliano, this information will be kept separate from our other medical file due to the highly sensitive nature of it. We encourage you to see an HIV/AIDS Infectious Disease Specialist immediately upon your arrival in the United States. We regret to inform you that your medical testing indicates that you are HIV Positive.

He gasped and grabbed his chest and was struggling, having an extremely hard time, even to breathe, alarming Maggie. She quickly asked, "Are you all right? What's the matter? Do you think you're having a heart attack, my darling? Talk to me!"

Finally, he breathed out, "Get me a glass of water, my mouth is so dry."

Maggie called the stewardess and asked for the water, she quickly returned and asked if any further assistance was needed, Francis only nodded his head slowly, side to side indicating no. He needed help she couldn't give him. Maggie questioned him slowly, "Can you handle the reporters waiting for us? Should I have them give us an alternate exit?"

"Can you?"

"I need information. Help me to understand, Francis," almost begging. He handed her the letter and said, "I can't marry you. I won't infect the person I love." Maggie read the letter as he spoke to himself knowing she would hear.

"I just now found this addition to my medical record. It was kept separate from the rest. Maggie, please understand, were the words coming from his mouth as she put her cupped hand over his lips, "How did you become HIV positive? I want to start there, talk fast, we land in a half hour."

"How do most health care professionals get HIV?" he asked with disdain in his voice, "A dirty needle stick while I was in the field before the whole abduction occurred. I just knew when it happened, too. I forgot about it when everything started happening. Now I am a male nurse priest who is HIV positive," he thought out loud, "Widow Bridges is going to have a field day with this bit of information. She'll probably say I came here to blame it on Africa and tell all of the tabloids."

"Stop it," Maggie demanded, "Who cares what anybody thinks? I love you and I am going to marry you. We are still young enough to have an Angela or Frankie of our own. Don't take away my dream." Then the pilot announced overhead to prepare for landing. Francis and Maggie had no idea of the local fame they acquired while they were gone. There was a sea of people with cameras and microphones waiting for them, "Over here, no, over here," they shouted out to them as they walked off the plane.

The airport police kept the paparazzi back from the landing gate but many of the reporters had clearance passes that allowed them past security to congregate near the gate door. It seemed like all of the other passengers deplaned and scattered leaving Francis and Maggie to walk on to the baggage claim area alone except they weren't alone, they were surrounded by a mob. There was Angela and Dustin standing in the baggage claim area, thank God they came to pick them up but even they couldn't rescue them from this enthusiastically active and attentive media crowd, they couldn't even get near to them. As they watched and waited for their luggage to appear on the rotating wheel, they decided to tell the media, it was short and simple and they finished by saying they were relieved to be home and out of harm's way.

Chapter Twenty Two

What Did It All Mean Now?

Francis waved goodbye to Maggie and Angela when they dropped him off at the tired old rectory and Angela drove Maggie home to the convent. Once inside Francis could only thank God for the peace and quiet but as he thanked Him, the phone rang and rang and rang as he let the machine answer it."Welcome home, Frankie-boy, Mr. Newsmaker, I saw you on the national news earlier," it was his cousin, Joey. They grew up together but took notably different paths in life. Joe went on to become a famous rocknroll recording artist with a style like Eric Clapton, and knows what it's like first hand to deal with the media. Francis ran to pick up the phone and said, "Hey it's me! Just let the machine stop and then we'll talk," after they heard the beep, Francis cheered up and said, "It is so good to hear your voice!"

"Following you in the news is like, amazing! I just want you to know that people all over the world and all over this country love you. You are going to beat this thing. It's treatable here nowadays."

"I know. I just have to adjust to the idea that I am HIV positive. I need to be educated and now more than ever I want to educate people."

Joey hesitated then said, "Look – I remember when you and Maggie first dated, when the two of you worked at the hospital. We had a lot of fun and laughs back then and I was working hard to make it, you two were so in love – I can still see the two of you, so I am giving my advice whether it is asked for or not."

"Joey, what can I say? Okay shoot, you're a brother to me not just a cousin, you love me. What?" Francis asked desperately wanting to hear what he had to say.

"I watched Maggie today at the press conference that was set up for you at the airport, you know they broke into the regular program with Breaking News to show it, ya know, Mr. Big Stuff."

"Stop it already."

"She loves you, HIV and all. You're crazy if you put a hold on marrying her."

"Joe, you forget that I am still a priest. We have a lot to work out and maybe God..," but before Francis could say it, Joey interrupted him, "Maybe God, what? Gave this to you so you would remain celibate? Are you nuts? You're the Minister and I got to tell you about God! No, God didn't do that and He will make a way to help the two of you."

"Joe, I believe you are right, I just need time to think this thing through and to work it all out. The Bishop called me on the way home from the airport and wants to meet with me in the morning and I have a parish council meeting tomorrow night. I need time to process all of this information."

"Choose, Maggie! The hell with all of the rest of that! You love each other and that's all that matters. Meet me with her in Vegas and just get married."

"Oh, you think you're so funny! Besides when I do get married, I am having a church wedding and it will be at an altar before God and man."

"Excuse me, my padre, but I do like that you said, 'when' not 'if'. Say your prayers, go to bed and wake refreshed. Remember grandma sending us off to bed? Making the sign of the Cross over us? Okay, she's gone now so I want to take care of you. I need you. Stay strong. Bono notta." Francis smiled as he hung up the phone and did just what Joe told him to do.

Chapter Twenty Three

Is This For Real?

Francis finished his morning prayers when there was a knock on the door. He thought to himself, "It's 7:20 in the morning, who could that be? I have to say mass at 8:15 this morning." He pulled the drapes slowly so no one would see and looked down to the figure standing on the porch. Her grey eyes met his. It was Henrietta Bridges and she knew he had seen her. She looked meaner than ever to him although he wasn't sure if that was true or just his prejudice toward her. Now he *had* to go back and answer the door. "Did she have to come over and harass me before my day even begins?" he cringed.

"Hello, Mrs. Bridges, it's nice to see you in spite of all that has happened since our last encounter," what a pathetic attempt to appear happy to see her, he mused to himself.

"May I come in, Father Francis? What I have to say won't take long. I know you have a busy day ahead of you especially with all the press and people waiting for you at St. Rita's."

"Oh no, not again! I didn't know there were people waiting for me. I thought I settled that all last night at the airport news conference."

"Let me speak, Francis. I know we have had our differences in the past," and as she tried to speak she began to weep. Her weeping became more intense until she reached out with both arms and hugged him to his utter amazement, "Forgive me," she sobbed.

"Henrietta, of course I forgive you, but for what?"

"When you revealed your HIV Positive status to the world last night, I was so proud of you and your courage as you explained your need to postpone any plans with Maggie, that was a sacrifice of your love to her. I know you love her and she loves you, I could see her standing behind you and looking at you, she has real love for you and was so supportive of you. Something happened to me when you turned to her and embraced. Your head seemed to fall on her shoulder. She gently lifted it with her two fingers and kissed you. It was clean and beautiful. I soiled it, made it dirty in the past. I am so very sorry. I don't know what will hpapen with the two of you but I am starting a petition to have her returned to this parish." Francis leaned forward and embraced her, "I can't tell you how much this means to me and honestly, she and I have never done anything sinful." She blurted in, "Stop that talk! I know it and I have always known it. I just hated you because you were a true spiritual Christian, struggles and all. I wanted the respect people gave to you so my heart was bitter toward you." He tried to help her by saying, "Maybe I antagonized you with my smiling all the time. People say I am a phony but really sometimes I don't even know when I'm smiling." She laughed a little and said, "Do you think I am that shallow? My hate was deeper. I am going to tell you a secret. My son died of AIDS. When I flew out to care for him a few years ago, I never told you what he died from because I was so ashamed of him. Oh may God forgive me. I was ashamed of my own son and God punished me, Francis."

"No, Henrietta! Don't do that to yourself!" he pleaded. Widow Bridges peeled her mask off and said, "Francis, I am HIV positive. I thought I was using universal precautions when I cared for him. When I got home, Doctor Hanson felt I should be screened when I told him my son whom I was caregiver to died of AIDS, just as a precaution. I was mortified when the test results came back. People loved you, even in your depression. People don't like being with me. I was a lonely widow. My only child was dead and I was HIV positive. But now everything has changed, you gave me hope last night. When you encouraged everyone to be tested, I know you meant it because you love them. You weren't judging them. I have love for them, too, and I want to work with you. I brought something here for you."

"You have already given me strength for the day. What is this? Oh, my God! Oh, my sweet Jesus! Thank you! Thank you, Henrietta! A fifty thousand dollar check made out to FAWN. Henrietta, I love you and I mean that in the highest sense. You're the one who has the courage and grace and generosity this morning." She explained, "When you called Angela forward last night at the press conference to introduce your new foundation she explained the need for liquid nutrition used in conjunction with the antiretroviral medication, I wanted to be the first to give, your first charter member."

"You know something, I want you to be the first. This shows me that God is working on a miracle for FAWN." She hurried him along saying, "You better get over to the church. It is standing room only, it's been all over the news this morning and people are heeding your advice going to clinics across the country to be tested. All night, the FAWN website was visited by millions with people wanting to help you. They're saying something like, you broke the stigma barrier or at the least are making it possible for them to identify with you. You also have some heavy hitters who are going to endorse FAWN. Some of the greatest miracles come right out of our pain, Francis. Bye for now and we'll talk soon. We have a lot of work to do."

She gently kissed him on the face and turned away then she was gone. Francis wondered if it was a dream but the red lipstick he wiped off of his cheek as his reflection stared back at him in the mirror assured him it wasn't.

Chapter Twenty Four

FAWN, *Yes, Marriage, No*

Francis walked over to the big beautiful but tired old church with its four steepled spires and was taken aback by what his eyes saw. It was like the news media had set up camp at St. Rita's. He thought to himself, "This really isn't news so it must stem from intense public interest," not knowing what was set to befall them in a short time to come. Right when he walked into the back entrance near the vestibule he almost literally bumped into Bishop McHenny and couldn't help blurting out, "What are you doing here? Our meeting is at 10:00 this morning." Bishop McHenny was tall with graying temples and a kind face, he was quiet but powerful. Francis and he had a good relationship but he also had an agenda of his own right then telling Francis forthright, "FAWN, yes. Marriage, no." Francis agreed by nodding outwardly while knowing inwardly Maggie was still and always will be a real part of his future. Could he or would he marry her were the questions needing answers but just not right now, Francis had a lot of praying and thinking to do.

The Bishop continued, "I'm here now because I want to say this morning's mass with you. You have quite a worldwide platform in there this morning and I want to be supportive, I don't want you to make any foolish mistakes. I am afraid for you."

"Don't be afraid for me just pray for me." Something that Francis discovered from the recent past was by increasing his time spent in prayer alone his faith grew to overcome fear in all things large and small. His parched soul before used to wear him down but has now become quenched and inner strength had become second nature to him.

They dressed in silent prayer with a common love of their vocation and the bond of unity. Francis knew Bob McHenny for years and loved him but Bob was definitely part of the Catholic establishment. "Boy, this must be big for him to come here this morning. I wonder who it was that got to him," he thought to himself.

Stepping out into the opening procession with the altar boys ready to march down the aisle, Francis peered out and saw the church was packed. People were standing all along the back of the big church. Who were all these people? They were not all members of St. Rita's. The music began playing an upbeat hymn with the choir in place. He wondered who had done all the planning for this simple morning mass, then he saw her, it was Angela, she smiled brightly and mouthed the words, "Internet invite." She prepared the church for this large crowd by the responses she received electronically and with Dustin, her new beau supportively standing strong beside her, the handsome couple was beaming with pride. Francis couldn't help but scan the room for Maggie as he proceeded down the aisle, searching the crowds right and left amid the media and standing room only crowd, not an empty space could be seen. "Why didn't she come? I know she must have known about it!" he wondered but he wasn't to be disappointed. As he and Bishop McHenny approached the altar, there she was, first row, left side, first seat; she looked up at him, their eyes locked in place as she slowly, barely opening her mouth, silently formed the words, "Be not afraid."

The ceremony of the mass progressed with a bit more pageantry since the Bishop was concelebrating it. As Francis prepared to start his homily he noticed the beautiful stained glass windows in this old church seemed even more luminous as the sun's rays shone through them today coloring the magnificent plate of the Good Samaritan with its brilliant blues and reds reflecting on him as he solemnly rose to stand at the pulpit. The window was speaking to the people even before Francis spoke a word.

Francis began his homily explaining that the church as a whole was the Good Samaritan and the world was the injured person. He paralleled the Good Samaritan to a male nurse who dressed wounds on a home care visit, transfered a patient to the hospital and made sure the patient had insurance coverage, this soliloquy began to draw the congregation into the realm of the Spirit but when he outlined the FAWN program and its need for workers, they began to smile unanimously and felt the real joy they had for so long been missing. When he reaffirmed his commitment in the light of his new HIV status they felt their faith deepen and grow stronger as he related it to this timeless story. When he began to notice the cameras and the sounds of pictures being taken, it became obvious to him then that he really was on an international HIV/AIDS platform. He wasn't used to people applauding in his church, some were even lifting up cases of Ensure and Boost they had brought with them as donations, there were cases of liquid nutrition all across the front and sides of the church; a huge banner attached to the side wall read "Ensure for Africa". He openly noted all of this so the cameras would focus in on it all. As he concluded he asked for churches, schools, community organizations, businesses and any other group from across the street to around the world to hold 'can drives'.

"We can help those with AIDS in Africa from Cape Town to Cairo. The sick will gain weight, feel stronger and live longer," he declared, "FAWN needs corporate sponsors, celebrity endorsements, million dollar donors and five dollar donors. We need prayer warriors and grant writers. We can make a difference on a grand scale, we must make that difference." Everyone shouted "yes" loudly and applauded then suddenly their 'yes' turned into a loud gasp! Francis didn't know what was going on until he looked at the Bishop on the other side of the altar slumped over in his chair, his color was bluish and it was not coming from the reflection of the windows. Francis quickly removed his priest garments and ran over to him while his days in the ER flashed back to him in freeze frames as if it was just yesterday. Simultaneously Maggie leaped into action from the front row and ran to the Bishop. Together they laid him on the floor, expertly ripped open his clothing but he didn't respond to their desperate queries. Francis kept repeating loudly and quickly, "Bob, I know you can hear me, work with us, fight with us," as Maggie cried out for someone to call 911. The two of them began CPR while cameras flashed their exposition to the world.

You could hear them counting '3, 4, 5, breathe', then wait, then check the pulse. They were an extraordinary team of excellence, in sync and unified as one unit could be. Just when the ambulance arrived, Maggie cried out, "I can feel a pulse, Francis! Yes! Yes!" when Francis cried out at the same time, "Look his color is coming back. He's coming around! Look, Mags, we've saved him! Thank you,God!" All of the camera lenses in the church closed in on them focusing first on her face then on his. In what seemed like a split second, two firemen ran up the main aisle slinging a gurney and yelling for people to step aside, shouting, "what happened?" One fireman started the IV with 9% normal saline solution, "he's got a pulse of 68, irregular, blood pressure is 98/60, respiration at 14, we've got to get him out of here stat." A third fireman read the pulse ox at 89% wrote the information down then helped the other two place him on the stretcher as they darted out of the church and sped off to the hospital as quickly as they came, in an instant.

This sudden and unexpected ending to such a blissfully spiritual morning seemed surreal. What followed for Maggie happened so spontaneously, like in times of past crises, she found herself again in the comfort and refuge of Francis' arms. He was right there again as he always had been and she wasn't dreaming. It was a post traumatic stress moment, allowing herself to "feel" after the stress of what just happened, trying to process it all; feeling safe and looking up at Francis she remembered what did transpire there so quickly and felt the true love and pride that their friendship so deserved especially in knowing Bishop McHenny will survive because they thought on their feet together, this feeling quickly dissipated due to the trauma that this time the whole world saw them.

Somehow Francis finished the service, rushed off to the hospital thinking the media will have to wait for him but for now they have enough in words and pictures to feed their fevered audience.

Chapter Twenty Five

At the Hospital

Francis had to laugh as he sped toward the hospital with Maggie. It was like a caravan of news trucks. "This would be funny if the bishop's life wasn't at stake, Maggie, what are you doing? It sounds like you are mumbling." She stopped to explain, "I have something to tell you. When you were gone and I went on that Charismatic retreat, I was given the gift of tongues. Add another label to me, I guess you could call me a Catholic Charismatic so other groups of people can now be angry with me."

"Well, I have something to tell you," he replied rather quickly, surprising her.

"I'm all ears."

"When I was held captive and was desperately crying out to God, I received the gift of tongues, too, so at least the same group of folks will be mad at the both of us," he laughed, "I don't care about them though, it's like a new strength came into me and remained with me as I prayed in the Spirit. It renews my joy when I pray in the Spirit. I am grateful for this gift of the Holy Spirit."

"Me, too! When we don't know how to pray, the Holy Spirit prays through us. That is why I was praying in tongues for Bishop McHenny. I didn't really know what to pray for him."

"Let's pray together the rest of the way to the hospital and I know God will hear and answer our prayers," he said oblivious to the caravan behind them.

When Francis parked in the ER parking lot, he called out to the media guys saying, "We are praying for the Bishop. I am going in and I don't have any more to tell you than that."

The Admissions Clerk at the ER desk was well aware of who Francis was and immediately informed him, "The Bishop has been rushed to surgery to open some blockages in his coranary arteries. They told me to direct you to go up to the Cardiac Surgical Waiting Room." As Maggie and Francis were making their way to the waiting room, they decided to detour and take pause in the hospital chapel and quiet themselves, knowing the bishop would be in surgery for quite a while. As they both knelt and prayed, a sense of peace came over them both which passed their understanding. They knew the Bishop was still in danger but they knew God's will would be done. They sat and listened for the Spirit of God to give them direction. It came in a most mysterious way.

It seemed like the door was barged opened when they recognized the voice, "Oh Lord, help us," they heard. They shouted back, "Tracey!" their friend and coworker at the Bread of Life Food Bank, who is also a minister at Faith Church and a Chaplain at the hospital. They jumped up and hugged her, "We are so glad to see you!" Francis shouted.

Tracey was a little bit over five feet tall but stood tall in the spirit. She said, "I have been wanting to see you two. You've been all over the news and you've been driving Crazy Tracey even more crazy praying for you. The more I prayed for you, the more my heart grew for FAWN. I want to be your Coordinator, don't even try to tell me no. I am going to Africa with you next time you go and you know we are going soon. My friend, Ana, you know, the first grade teacher, she's already written a children's book to help educate the children and she wants to come, too. She hopes to bring a high school team with her someday, call it a Service Learning Project!"

"I love it! I know you! And I trust you! All this media hoopla has thrown me for aloop. I need to get grounded and work with the people I know," Francis excitely exclaimed.

"You need some color on that board, too. My people are from Africa and I have to do something to help with the AIDS crisis there, too. Oprah isn't the only sister going and doing something there!" her huge smile radiated the entire room.

"I remember meeting Ana at Bread of Life. She is Hispanic. What caused her to catch the vision?" Francis asked honestly.

"The Holy Ghost, Francis. She leads intercession at the church and it was told to her through somebody who prophesied over her that she'd write the book and go with us. It was confirmed inside of her, she knew it was right. It's God, Francis, God is in this FAWN thing. We just hear His voice and just listen and we proceed. Ana and I are going to help you. Right, Sister Maggie? Just nod your head, yes. You know I'm going to tell you like it is." Tracey never missed a beat in explaining anything of what she needed to say. Maggie knew to nod in the affirmative. Tracey went on, "My eight year old son, Josiah, he thinks FAWN is a city. He wants to be the Mayor of FAWN someday. Isn't that too much?"

"Tracey, I'm feelin' it," Francis said, "Let's plan to meet and go forward with this. Right now we have to get up to the

Surgical Waiting Room. Call the rectory and make an appointment for us to meet and plan right there in the kitchen, eating and planning." Tracey waived her hand at them, "Go, go! I'll be talkin' to you. Let's enjoy the FAWN ride! God's got a plan and I want to be right in the center of it!"

Maggie and Francis entered the waiting room and quickly found their seats, settled in and looked up and there they were hugging on the TV, right under the magnificent crucifix which was artfully and beautifully suspended over the altar of the church as the Bishop was sped away by ambulance after together they truly saved his life.

Chapter Twenty Six

Loves Got Everything to Do With It

The days sped by and Bishop McHenny reached full recovery but something very real began happening for Francis. First he noticed quite quickly a change in church attendance. People were coming to church regularly and continued coming and new people were joining. The people related to him whether they were young, old, black, white, brown, red, yellow, this new congregation was truly diverse. All three Sunday services were packed with standing room only and his weekday morning masses were very well attended. The publicity obviously didn't hurt but something else was going on that Francis couldn't put his finger on.

One day while he was praying and preparing his sermon he seemed to have a spiritual awakening and thought to himself, "Loves got everything to do with it. How simple, yet I didn't get it before. I tried programs and campaigns and festivals but they only drew a crowd. Those things didn't keep them." Francis was unaware of his utter transparency. He felt he had nothing to hide and opened his heart to the people. Face it, he loved a woman he couldn't marry, at least for the time being. He was HIV positive, he stared death in the face in Africa and grew stronger with God's grace. Everyday was a gift to him. He wasn't afraid of the sick and oppressed, love removed any fear.

Most of his prayer life changed. He would plead with God, "Let me love your people for you today. Make something special happen to let love and joy flow from my heart to theirs." Those special moments began to occur a lot more frequently than he knew, sometimes he was operating in a love exchange that even he was unaware of.

He sincerely invited the HIV/AIDS community to come nearer and be healed. He invited the brokenhearted and lonely, the addicted and greedy, and those from the other side of the tracks and discovered both sides were there. He compelled the parishioners to bring their sick. In the front of the church, he removed the first three rows of pews for those in wheelchairs and stretchers. He appealed to caregivers to bring the dying for what might possibly be the last service they will ever attend. He still made his hospital rounds and home visitations but desired the church family to be together on Sunday, if possible, like a natural father wanting his family around the table. He invited and invited and invited and they came and came and came for the Sunday spiritual meal. Many stayed the entire day and enjoyed the wonderful pot luck natural dinner feast, all the while, all in all they experienced wholeness and feeling the love of community.

Francis began to dream at night about how to love God's children more, then he learned what he had to do as an answer to some of his prayers. He turned the rectory into an AIDS hospice which would house the elderly and the dying. He didn't waste anytime contacting his old friend, Josephine, who was an Administrator for a local nursing home for the last two decades, she knew top to bottom how to organize and manage this. She only asked that he not forget the mentally ill and developmentally challenged, she knew of an empty house nearby where they could set up an establishment to serve the children of God with special needs and requirements, the ones who are typically overlooked on a day to day basis which around the country and the world painted the bleak picture of hopelessness rather than planting the seeds of faith, hope and love. Josephine had the perfect manager for the two homes, Maya. The second Francis said he'd love to meet Maya, the plans were set in motion and real progress began to develop.

Tracey and Henrietta were working together wonderfully on setting up the first FAWN shipment with Dave at Gateway Shipping. One thousand cases of Ensure and Boost were shipped to Brother Isaac in Johannesburg, South Africa. St. Paul's Church pioneered the effort, they set a pattern for other churches across the country and fielded the calls that came in – answering all the 'how to' questions. People were so generous in donating their funds and holding 'can drives'. 'Just ask Lois at St. Paul's' was the mantra whenever a question arose that couldn't be answered.

Francis was being educated about HIV/AIDS in a very personal way. A nurse at the Health System AIDS Clinic named Kam made contact with him out of true concern, she saw him wearing himself out in each story that broke in the media. When Kam called he could tell she really cared about him by the compassion in her voice and he agreed to meet with her at the clinic. He felt strange going to the sterile white clinic but Kam wore a warm smile when she greeted him and as he put out his hand to shake hers, she pulled him in to a warm embrace, "Thanks for all the good you're doing to get the word out," she said, "Let me help you." Then she explained the need for his beginning and staying on antiretroviral therapy in combination with proper rest, proper diet and healthy living for the rest of his life. Francis admitted that he is a nurse who needs to be educated in this area, he understood that what he now learned could save his life and he would share it with others.

Did he feel well enough to go to Africa and meet the next shipment? It would arrive there in 52 days. He didn't feel well that particular day, he was somewhat weak and tired, flu-like. But so many lives depended on him and he kept positively reinforcing himself that maybe tomorrow he would feel stronger. He couldn't afford to get an opportunistic infection. How would he keep all these plates spinning? All he knew was he had to get home and get into bed.

Chapter Twenty Seven

HIV Becomes AIDS

He told himself, "I'll feel better tomorrow." a little time had passed and wonderul things had taken place but it seemed like his tomorrows had run out. There he lay in that white and cold and most of all lonely hospital bed at 3:00 AM listening to the beeping of the machines around him. How did he get so sick? Sick to the point of being near death? He knew it was his fault he just wouldn't listen to anyone's strong advice when they told him, "Don't go to Africa a fourth time," they said, "let the others take the burden off you." He didn't listen to his body or his doctors and most of all to Maggie; he kept telling himself, "People need me. It's all about the love, love which lays down its life for others. But still I should have listened and heard, but it can't be that this is the end and not the beginning, they need more from me, I have to be able to give it to them. Am I dying, Lord?"

It was like his life was passing before him. His mind drifted to stories from his second trip to Africa when the liquid nutrition was delivered to the FAWN partnering church scheduled to be distributed that afternoon. People were lined up, the place was filling up to capacity and up on the altar were decoratively wrapped cans. The children from a U.S. vacation bible school made them, they wrote messages of love on the cans with pictures of flowers and hearts. The simple messages said prayers were being offered and good thoughts were being sent. A mother and her seven year old daughter went up to the altar platform to publicly thank the FAWN team and declared that she was HIV positive but determined to beat this devastating disease. Her seven year old daughter took the microphone, she tried to speak from her heart but couldn't get the words out from crying so hard. Then one of the ladies on the team ran to her and held and hugged her tightly. It was the first of many tender moments. Francis remembered looking around that room and feeling the love that day and thinking to himself, "This is what it is all about, I'm living my purpose." Next Francis immediately remembered and thought back about another person very ill from AIDS. His name was Alfred, he was too sick to come to the church and pick up his 'little tins', as he liked to call them so the team delivered them to him. Francis would picture it all in his mind just as if it were happening right now before his eyes. He even whispered out loud, "he was the whole reason for that trip." Of course other people and things were also very important but the reaffirmation for FAWN was found in Alfred. Whenever Francis thought of Alfred he would always remember the Book of John, Chapter Four, Verse 7, "God is love and he that loves is born of God and knows God." I always wanted FAWN to be known by its love of God and love of neighbor and in Alfred it was; the love and light of God shined brightly in him.

Once Francis and a few volunteers were asked by Margaret, the church leader over the FAWN project there to follow her with a couple of the sisters to Alfred's dwelling. The village was not safe and the team was stared down several times by hostile eyes but they continued steadfast on their mission. Francis was not afraid but knowing what danger smelled like he remained vigilant and aware of protecting the small group not wanting anyone to get hurt. He recorded in his journal that evening, "I felt like Jesus walking with the twelve

through Samaria, those Samaritan's didn't like Him either."
Francis could remember every detail. When they got to
Alfred's tiny two room house, he was lying in his bed in the
back room, the house was musty, dirty and hot. As Alfred
tried to prop himself up to greet the kind and compassionate
visitors, Francis embraced him as he helped him to a sitting
position. Alfred could speak only in a whisper and with
small gasps, "I was receiving the tins, was strong enough to
go to church, then they ran out and so did I. I [got] weaker
and weaker, couldn't get out the bed...then heard the tins had
arrived...I was too sick to go to the church...thank you for
bringing them to me." Alfred was too weak to hold the can to
his mouth so Francis held him up with one arm behind his
back and a can of Ensure in the other holding it to his lips
giving him small mouthfuls, then gently laid him back down
and Alfred said, "Please pray for me." The team gathered
around him and after praying for a few minutes a soft light
filled the room and Alfred's eyes danced serenely as he
softly spoke, "Jesus, Jesus is here. I feel Him." Here the
mission became validated. Alfred received the love of a
nurse and servants and the love of God shined through and
on him and everyone in the room.

Suddenly Francis' attention came back into the hospital
room where he lay as he thought, "I've had a rich life, very
rich, so what if I die?" he felt some sense of satisfaction but
not totally convinced he finished his race. Since he returned
from that first trip to Africa the parish had taken off and was
thriving, people were truly being fed spiritually and their
lives were changing, the bills were paid, "Now that's a
miracle!" he chuckled to himself, "happy people and no
debt."

An associate, Fr. John, was assigned to help him. Francis
knew John and thought he was great and he was delighted to
have company in the small basement apartment they shared
in the rectory since it was modified into a hospice and senior
assisted living center upstairs. Francis, of course, worked all

hours of the day and night, visiting dying patients to nurse them and pray with them. Sometimes he would get a call at 2:00 AM in the morning because a dementia patient or psychiatric patient escaped and couldn't be found, Francis somehow could always find them. He smiled at these recollections and was grateful for all the graces in his life and in thanksgiving he would say, "Dear Lord, thank You that nobody ended up missing again today." Day in and day out he was the servant of all.

FAWN was spreading up the African continent and many sufferers of AIDS were being given the nutrition they needed. A brother named Johnny was running the African office of FAWN. Johnny was busy with volunteer student groups for the distribution of the cans of nutrition in several African nations. His heart of compassion was like an extension of Francis' heart. Francis smiled as he thought of Johnny visiting the many villages and sending pictures of himself dressed in colorful African clothing. While corporate sponsors and celebrity endorsements helped to provide the steady funding needed to support the program, Johnny's efforts helped build good will and expand it. Frankie, Libby and little Frankie Jr. continued with their medical mission work and linked up with Johnny and FAWN. Discussions began with leaders of China, India and Russia to bring FAWN there to help with the increasing AIDS epidemic. Who would've thought all this would develop?

He smiled thinking back on Angela and Dustin's wedding. In one way, Francis felt he should have walked Angela down the aisle but instead he was pleased to have performed the wedding. He saw the joy on Angela's face as Dustin placed the beautiful gold wedding band on her finger, now it means more to him to have presided over their vows than walking her down the aisle. Today they are the proud parents of little Julian, the name of the college where Maggie and Francis first met. "How sweet is that?" he smiled and mused when thinking of Angela teaching Julian to call him Grandfather Francis instead of Father Francis.

As wonderful as all of these things were he now has one more thing to resolve to put his house in order in case he passes away and that's Maggie. She faithfully and tirelessly worked with him throughout the past five years. A lot of these successes were because of her and they shared them together but not as husband and wife. Something was lacking even as good as everything was. Francis was going to do the right thing before he died, he had to and that's all there was to it. He thought back to when he visited the pope in Rome to discuss the church's role in caring for those with AIDS in Africa, the discussion was infected with the topic of celibacy or the marriage of the religious, the subect of AIDS got a somewhat cold reception. But something changed in Francis upon his return from the papal visit, he was honored by the invitation to Rome and the support for FAWN but the fact that Maggie wasn't invited continued to eat at him. He could feel her wounded heart and told her, "I'll make it up to you," she smiled warmly and said, "do you think that really matters to me? They can try to keep us apart physically but you know this love triangle I have lived in is not going to beat me. So what if the other woman is the Church? I refuse to have a jealous spirit. I know you love me."

Those words stung him to the core as he lay in that hospital bed with the ticking clock obnoxiously counting every beat of his heart making it loudly echo as each second went by increasing his dull anxiety. He never looked at it that way before until she said those words, "I guess they do call it, Mother Church," he bristled in thought, "I finally realize what game we've been playing and Maggie knew it all the time."

It was after the return from Rome when his body weakened and his spirit followed. The high fever and the pneumonia were complications of his compromised immune system. He believed if he made it right with Maggie his spirit would revive and so would his body. He picked up the phone, "3:00 in the morning or not", he said to himself, "before I die, I am going to marry Maggie, nothing else matters now." His plan was to marry her before God but not in a Catholic Church. Even as he felt his life slowly slipping away he pressed the keys on his cell phone. The phone rang and rang, then Francis heard what he wanted to hear, "Hello, Francis, is everything okay?" his friend, Pastor Craig,a minister and a doctor, had his name programmed in his phone so he would always know who was calling. He told Francis to call him any time of day or night, that he would be there for him always, he would never forget what a friend Francis was to him during a very dark time in his own life. Coincidentally they first met at the local ministerial association when they were both new to the city and answered their call to serve God at the same time, there they had a common bond although they were from different denominations, but they knew they were compatible the instant they discovered they're both from medical backgrounds.

"Can you come to the hospital first thing in the morning, Pastor Craig? I need a minister."

Chapter Twenty Eight

Oprah's Nod

People began to gather and assemble outside of his hospital window. The media carried the news that Father Francis was failing. The public reaction was a surprise to Francis after he had settled into loving people one day at at time whether here or in Africa, the media had left him alone it seemed. There was the occasional story and once a tabloid screamed the headline, 'Sister Maggie's Pregnant with Father Francis' AIDS Infected Baby', but things were noticeably quieter now. The tabloid headline was a joke to them not worthy of any reaction especially since there was no truth to it. Maggie's response only cemented Francis' feeling towards her, "I'd carry your child even if he or she were HIV positive." The best thing about the sporadic publicity was that it helped to keep the funds flowing into FAWN and his appearance on The Oprah Show was perfect, too, since they shared a common concern for AIDS in Africa.

Oprah introduced Maggie and invited her to join them on the show, she couldn't help but ask them about their love life but she handled it with grace and with the determination and balance that she is known for. She always has her special moments though, when she found out through Maggie and Tracey that Francis' theme song for FAWN brings tears to his eyes everytime he hears it, to his utter amazement and pure delight, Oprah introduced Stevie Wonder who performed, 'There a Place in the Sun', Francis teared up as the song continued, 'where there's hope for everyone.' The Oprah Show was a highlight but things eventually settled down. The show was aired shortly after his return from his fourth trip to Africa. All he knew for certain was that he was so extremely tired when he returned.

No one thought it would progress into pneumonia. He was weakening and his associate, Father John noticed that Francis was not breathing properly. He was taking short shallow breaths when he collapsed. John called 911 and Francis was admitted to Doctors Hospital. Instead of getting stronger, he was getting weaker. Maggie would visit daily and saw his condition worsening. Even though she is a nurse, it is always difficult caring for a loved one. The shocking news when she was told that he would be transferred to the ICU and placed on a ventilator soon was a bitter pill for her to swallow.

He was in a private room with a window, the hospital was trying to respect his privacy but even so he could feel people passing by his door in a slow yet seemingly steady stream, peering in and offering a gentle smile. Maggie was his Medical Durable Power of Attorney and he told her he desired not to be put on a ventilator. He said, "If it's my time to go, let me go be with the Lord. No heroic life saving measures." Maggie would stroke his hair and take a damp wash cloth to his face. He would smile at her and mouth the words, "thank you". Maggie wouldn't cry in front of him so she focused intensely on his care until one day she couldn't help it. That was the day he knew he had to make things right which resulted in his call to Pastor Craig.

Francis counted on Maggie's faithful visits. Sure enough the day came when she arrived and began to straighten up the room and comb his hair. Francis found the strength to reach into the bed table drawer beside him and pulled out a small navy blue jewelry box lined with light blue satin. Seeing the satin cloth as he opened it, Maggie then saw the engagement ring he had given her on Christmas Eve so long ago. Francis said with a whisper, "Please take it. If I do go, I want you to have it. It's always belonged to you. Forgive me, if you can for the road I've had you travel on with me. If I have hurt you in any way, I must know that you forgive me." Maggie began to weep and covered her face with her hands. It took her a moment to speak, "I wanted you to give it to me as a symbol of our future life together not like this," then pausing she said, "I will take it and cherish it. I will always keep it in the box and I know I will open it periodically to feel you near, for comfort, strength and love. Just please don't die. Please. I don't care that we weren't married, we shared a rich life. I want to keep on sharing it, we need to keep on sharing it." Then Francis spoke softly saying, "I don't think you understand me. I am asking you to marry me. Pastor Craig was here this morning and is coming back at 3:00 this afternoon. We will be married by a minister of the Gospel just not a Catholic priest. Maggie, we are going to be married before God. I don't have a lot of time left and this is a wrong I must right. Will you marry me?" Maggie was stunned. She thought this part of their past was never to be dealt with again even as Francis' condition worsened. He told her about his 3 AM call to Pastor Craig and his agreement to perform the private ceremony. Francis further explained there would be no license since he was too sick to get one but assured her they would be man and wife before God. He explained by saying, "Maggie, to save you the hassle when I am gone, there will be no legal record. You can continue to be a nun. Pastor Craig will provide a certificate from his church that you will always have as a record of this day." She went from sadness to joy to sadness. "Yes, ten thousand times, yes. Let's just do it this time," she looked at herself and said, "I am going home and changing. I am not getting married looking like this." Francis smiled and said, "Be back by 3:00." She kissed his lips with a passion reserved for lovers and said so sweetly, "I love you."

Chapter Twenty Nine

I Do

It was a beautiful ceremony which Pastor Craig kept short but Maggie's appearance made it really special. She wore a pure white dress with just a touch of lace at the hem. It was simple to the knee, gathered slightly at the waist with pearl buttons on the cuffs of the blouson sleeves. She wore silky white nylons and white open toed shoes with heels. Her hair was neatly pulled back with loose tendrils framing her face and neck with fresh baby's breath spaced ever so perfectly in her hair and a wristband with pink and white spray roses, lavendar larkspur and beaded pearl chiffon ribbon. She was radiant, her eyes sparkled with joy. She was the most beautiful bride Francis had ever seen and he had perfomed a lot of weddings. Angela and Dustin served as the witnesses. Angela was smiling and crying at the same time, "How can I have joy and tears together?"

This was Top Secret. The door was closed and the drapes were drawn. Only God and five people were meant to know. Francis felt there were a multitude of angels in the room. Those present were given the privilege of hearing Francis' faint "I do" and watch him put the ring on Maggie's trembling finger. They heard Maggie tenderly say, "I do" as she bent over to kiss the groom. Pastor Craig pronounced them husband and wife and blessed the rings in the name of the Father, the Son and the Holy Spirit. They were finally married and there was love, peace and joy in the room.

Paster Craig left the room wondering if that would be the last time he would ever see his friend alive, and held back tears as Maggie thanked him again. Angela and Dustin embraced the newlyweds kissing each of them on the cheek, Angela was really choked up but able to say, "I've waited a long time for this, now the circle is complete. We'll leave you alone. See you tomorrow." Maggie stayed another half hour then told Francis she wanted him to rest. The day was very emotional and rest was the best thing for him. She kissed him and said, "Goodbye, my husband," and he replied, "Goodbye, my wife."

The night was long and difficult for Francis, his condition deteriorated rapidly, his breathing became increasingly more laborious. The antibiotics weren't touching the pneumonia and the decision of the ventilator had to be made. Maggie was summoned to the hospital at about 4:00 in the morning. Francis arguably nodded his head "no" to Maggie's fierce insistence that he start on a ventilator to help him to breathe. The doctor told Maggie because of his refusal of further treatment, the only thing they could recommend now was hospice care which Francis agreed to when Maggie told him. His only request was to go home to the hospice at the rectory. He never thought the hospice he developed would serve him one day or at least not so soon.

It was 6:00 a.m. now and Maggie called Maya, the hospice manager, at home. She hadn't left work and Maggie wanted to ask her if she would meet her at the rectory in an hour. Maggie finally lost it and began to sob on the phone to Maya, "Francis is being placed on hospice and wants to..." sobbing with tears, Maya could feel it through the phone, "...to come back to the rectory as a hospice patient...they say it's a matter of time, maybe a few days." Maya, having had a lot of experience in helping people with their final journey reassured Maggie by saying, "I know this is hard. I will receive him as a true gift, oh, all of the staff will make it so special. I will play spiritual music and his Connie Francis Italian songs that he loves so much." Maggie felt lighter for that brief moment and said, "See you within the hour." Maya called ahead to the staff at the rectory hospice, locked her door and sped away with grace and dignity, setting aside her own feelings now while praying non stop for God's guidance and direction of how to give comfort to the dying Francis and his traveling companion and best friend, Maggie.

When Maya walked into the hospice the staff was preparing Francis' room. His favorite pictures were on the wall and music was playing when the ambulance arrived with Maggie's car right behind it. Francis was laid in his bed with every comfort available, the oxygen flowed through his nasal passages, his hospital bed was upright, but the light blue pajamas he wore matched his coloring because his blood wasn't oxygenating properly, his energy level was so low that it took every muscle and ounce of energy he had in him to speak. He could still somewhat turn his mouth into a smile, kindly smiling at each person as they expressed their love to him, he even acknowledged Connie Francis singing 'Mama' as the CD player sending its message of passion throughout the room but all he could do was shake his head slightly and smile at Maya.

The church next door became crowded and full as people gathered day and night for a candlelight vigil. Their singing was soft and inspirational, the hymns gave them faith and comfort. Individuals began sharing how their lives were changed and enriched under Francis' ministry. Some shared their HIV status and the courage Francis had given them. They encouraged everyone there to be tested and know their status so if necessary they could be treated and prevent the spread of the disease. It was all about love, the love they first received and felt and this love they wanted to share and give back. They never stopped praying for a miracle for Francis but his condition was worsening by the hour. Maggie wouldn't leave his bedside. She had been up for nearly 24 hours. It was now 3:00 in the morning. She didn't think he'd make it through the night and she was right. Francis had one final request, in spite of his weakness he was able to hold up his index finger.

"What? What?" Maggie asked desperately wanting to know what he needed in these last moments hoping she could fulfill whatever it was reminding herself in great sorrow this would be the last time she could be there for him when he needed her.

"Henrietta Bridges," he breathed out heavily, "I must see her. I could never forgive her," he breathed out slowly, "for all the pain she caused us." The name of the woman that caused so much pain to them both and others subject to her cruelty was most unexpected as Maggie sat with her ear close to his mouth intensely listening so she could understand his muffled words. To avoid anymore stress in asking him to explain further on the subject, she told him, "She knows you forgive her."

"I must tell her. Please get her. I forgive her", each breathe was a separate agony, "I...do...love her...I would never really...let her...work...with me...in FAWN...I held a grudge...before...I die...I...want...to see...her." Maggie sprang into action, left the room and stood in the hallway trying to reach Henrietta on her cell phone but there was no answer, she let the phone ring twenty times in desperation, hung up and waited five minutes before trying again but Henrietta's phone just kept ringing. Maggie whispered into the phone, "Wake up, wake up, Henrietta, please God, let her wake up". But it just rang. No answer. Maggie went back into the room to tell Francis she was trying hard to reach her but couldn't.

"Please, Maggie." Francis gasped.

Maggie went back out into the hallway and tried again. Finally Henrietta heard her phone vibrating on her bedside stand and answered it, "Hello, Maggie. No, I've tried to sleep but can't. I've been watching it on the news. I was at the church earlier. He wants me? I know he loves me and yes, I know he forgives me. I know, I know. We settled that long ago. I love him. I really do. Tell him I am coming. I will be right over."

When Maggie walked back into his room, the instrumental hymn of Amazing Grace was heard playing softly but something was really wrong, his breathing had changed, it was worse if that were even possible. "Henrietta's on her way. Hold on if you can, try to hold on. I am here, my darling." Time was ticking rapidly on, then like lightning she realized she had to let him go, "It's okay to go, my love," then softly said, "I gave Henrietta your message." She gently sat near to him and held his hand in hers. "I will be reunited with you one day," his mouth barely moving as the words traveled into her ear so close to his mouth with his last dying breath, then he was gone. Maggie sat for a long time and watched the mystery of life unfold before her, staring at him and believing the reality that now there was nothing she could ever do for him again, nothing she could do to bring him back to life. She gently slipped the precious wedding band she had given him off his finger and placed it in her pocket.

Chapter Thirty

The Threshold of Hope

Something was different in the room now, there was a warm glow surrounding it. Maggie had no idea what was going on in the realm of the Spirit but she felt an indescribable peace. The hospice workers called the police to come and verify the hospice death. The police arrived, verified the death, then made the call to the coroner, as pre-arranged. Francis' body was beginning to cool down as life started to leave it but his spirit was alive outside of his body. He floated out of his body and saw everything that was taking place, he looked at the clock, it was exactly 4:00 a.m. He saw Maggie but she could not see him, he tried to comfort her but she could not hear him. He was saying, "Maggie, I am okay. Don't worry about me."

Then suddenly he noticed a magnificent eight foot tall radiant angel standing next to him with two large beautiful fluffy wings emerging from his back. He looked fiercely strong yet love emanated from within and without surrounding his entire being. He spoke to Francis saying, "It's time to go, I will escort you on your flight into the presence of God." Francis looked at him as if he knew and nodded agreeing, "Are you my Guardian Angel?" The angel smiled at him and said, "Yes, I have been with you always."

Just before they were to enter a tunnel of light, Henrietta Bridges barged into the hospice room and grabbed Maggie in a tight bear hug and sobbed uncontrollably. Francis took note of her and felt a sudden flush of compassion for her and remarked, "I do love her, I do." Henrietta knelt and wept over Francis' body and declared her love to him, "I always loved you even when I felt you excluded me. I knew I had hurt you deeply. I knew you forgave me from your heart but your mind got in the way, that's all, yet love can transcend the mind."

Francis turned his gaze up toward the light following it and then entered into the tunnel. His angel was behind him as they traveled through space toward Heaven. He could hear music, the music of Heaven. It was so beautiful and so inviting, caressing him. The fragrance of heavenly flowers entered the tunnel and enriched all of his senses. He could see the colors of Heaven, pastels were everywhere. But it was the light that drew him. There also was a brilliant light that enveloped the individuals waiting at the end of the tunnel, the light was magnificent and wondrously bright but it didn't hurt his eyes, he felt sure that one of them was Jesus, His image appeared infinitely more splendid than the paintings and statues depicted of His likeness on Earth with His arms stretched out in an inviting pose. But who was that other person and the people behind them?

It was Alfred from Africa! Alfred's death was unknown to Francis. Francis heard Jesus say, "What you've done to the least, you've done to me." Francis saw his mother and father there smiling and waving at him, they looked so young. He saw his Auntie Jean and his grandmother, too. Behind them there was a myriad of other people that Francis had loved in his life's journey, there were too many to count. "Francis," Jesus said, "I want you to hear and listen to what is going on there on Earth. People loved you because you loved them for me, people you didn't even know, you loved them for me. Thank you." Francis began to tune in to Earth and heard the media eulogizing him using wonderful descriptions of love and caring, "People from around the world had been touched by this simple man who loved all people, they loved him for it, they wanted to give it back to him and when he was afflicted, they felt his pain". As he listened, he wished them to know they were giving back. Unspeakable joy filled glory was all he felt until something strange started happening.

He began to listen again and heard sharply the familiar voices of those who gathered around his death bed. Maggie, Henrietta, Angela and Dustin were given complete and total privacy before the body would be taken away. Maggie was having a difficult enough time with her own grief while trying to comfort Henrietta, pulling her away and asking her to accept Francis' death, "We must go now, let's go in peace now, Henrietta." Angela and Dustin were trying to tell her, "It's going to be okay, Mrs. Bridges. Let's go." Henrietta was a strong woman for her age, she pulled herself free from them, went over to the body and knelt at his feet. Maggie, Angela and Dustin could only look on in pity, giving her a final chance to grieve. What they saw next defied all reason and amazed them because in an instant Henrietta began to cry out to God for Him to raise Francis from the dead. She boldly declared, "Jesus, sweet Jesus, You are the Resurrection and the Life, raise him up as You raised Lazarus from the dead, raise up our dear brother Francis, because we need him, so many others still need him, You know his work isn't done here. You welcomed my only son into your kingdom once before, Your joy in welcoming him was my real sorrow, mothers shouldn't bury their children, please make it so this my son, Francis, is only sleeping, raise him, please, so we can carry on the work and the dream. Please! WE LOVE YOU and THANK YOU!" Then she stood up and her continence changed.

Maggie was spellbound. She couldn't believe what she was seeing. Henrietta walked over to the head of the bed and pointed her finger at the lifeless body of Francis then shouted a loud declaration not a humble supplication and said, "Jesus said greater works than He would we do but only in His Name," she commanded the spirit of life to return to Francis' body through the divinity of our Lord, Jesus Christ, "Life return to Francis! In the name of the Father and the Son and the Holy Spirit". Maggie, Angela and Dustin had just about enough of this, Maggie couldn't even finish her words when curiousity piqued her attention to glare at Francis laying on the bed.

At Heaven's portal, Jesus turned to Francis and said, "She came boldly to the throne of Grace. She asked and it will be granted unto her. This time *I* can say *her* faith has made *you* well!", His smile was as bright as the sun and His laughter like a trickling brook, "You have to go back. Your work isn't done. You have begun to develop strong faith inside of people on Earth and I honor their faith and your life's work. You must go back to finish what I designed for you and you will be totally healed to do the work."

"Jesus", Francis humbly asked, "Do I have to go back? It is so beautiful here, so perfect."

Jesus smiled and embraced him, "My brother, I have prepared a mansion for you here in the New Jerusalem and one day you will return to it. Right now you have a new bride waiting for you to return to her on Earth, love conquers death. You will continue working together to complete the work." In a breath and the wink of an eye, Francis was gone.

Life re-entered his body and his eyes filled with tears and light. He began stretching his arms and legs and wiggling his toes. Then he sat up. Maggie, Angela, Dustin and Henrietta took several steps back in fear and shock. He said to Maggie, "I am so hungry. Do you have anything to eat?"

"Eat!? Eat?!" Maggie rushed to the head of the bed, slightly pushing Henrietta out of the way. She began touching his face and hands, they were warm again, "You're alive! Oh, my God!"

Henrietta opened the door and started hysterically screaming, "A miracle! It's a miracle, I tell you!" Maya and her staff, the policeman, and the coroner who hadn't even seen Francis yet, came running toward her. Trying to catch her breath, tone down her voice and keep her pounding heart from beating out of her chest, Henrietta was gasping as she slowly exclaimed, in almost a whisper, "it...it...it's a miracle.... Francis has returned to life." Maya quietly kept repeating to herself, "It's a miracle, I am witnessing a miracle." Henrietta left the hospice praising God, she went to the people in the church and to the media gathered nearby to tell them everything like only she could.

Back in his room, Francis got up and walked to the window, he waved to the people who had been gathered there for hours, they began cheering and screaming and some even fainted. He turned to Maggie and said, "Maggie," a little sternly, "take that ring out of your pocket." Wondering how he knew it was in her pocket, she retrieved it and slowly handed it to him. He held it up to look at it first before slowly slipping it on to the ring finger of his left hand. "Maggie, Jesus said he brought us together and nothing is ever going to separate us again. He said we are to complete our work together as man and wife." Maggie put her arms around her husband's waist and rested her head against his chest feeling more secure than she had ever felt in all of her life.

Their life together had only just begun.

The End of Book One.

Acknowledgments

I am grateful for all the help in creating this work.

Thank you to Ken Hammer for getting the ball rolling and then letting go gracefully. Thank You to Thaya McNivens and Fran Jensen for helping me begin the editing process. Special thanks to Jane Cortez for seeing the editing process to completion and helping me finish the work.

Thank you to my real life daughter Angela and her real life husband Dustin and their son, my grandson, Julian. They really are there for me. Thank you to my real life son, Dr. Frankie Julian and his wife Libby. I've enjoyed this journey sharing it with them.

Thank you to my many friends and my church family, who had to hear me talk this through and then supported me to it's completion.

Thank You to my Maggie in real life, my wife Peggy. Thank you to her for helping me write my life's story.

Thank you to all the supporters of FAWN throughout the years. Please visit the FAWN website and become more aware of what has already been done. The future of FAWN is awaiting it's manifest destiny. www. fightingaids.org